MUTT'S PROMISE

MUTT'S PROMISE

JULIE SALAMON

illustrated by **Jill Weber**

DIAL BOOKS FOR YOUNG READERS

DIAL BOOKS FOR YOUNG READERS
PENGUIN YOUNG READERS GROUP
An imprint of Penguin Random House LLC
375 Hudson Street
New York, NY 10014

Library of Congress Cataloging-in-Publication Data
Salamon, Julie.
Mutt's promise / Julie Salamon ; illustrated by Jill Weber.
pages   cm
Summary: "When their owner moves away, two dogs are trapped
in a puppy mill until they take matters into their own hands"—Provided by publisher.
ISBN 978-0-525-42778-0 (hardback)
[1. Dogs—Fiction. 2. Human-animal relationships—Fiction.
3. Survival–Fiction.] I. Weber, Jill, illustrator. II. Title.
PZ7.S1474Mu 2016   [Fic]—dc23
2015015747

Printed in the United States of America

1 3 5 7 9 10 8 6 4 2

Designed by Jill Weber
Text set in ITC New Baskervile

To our mothers,
Lilly Salcman & Barbara Schwartz,
with love and gratitude

CONTENTS

MUTT'S PROMISE

chapter one

BRAVE DOG

A striking golden-red dog ambled up the road, her long tail hoisted like a sail. She drifted through the thick summer air at a calm, steady pace. Though she once had a happy home, she was now on her own, unafraid to face her future—whatever it might be.

As the evening light shimmered in the heat, she gazed toward the setting sun, enjoying the sense of peace that had settled on this rolling stretch of countryside. It was quiet except for the mooing of distant cows. Then, with the ferocity of a lightning crack, the spell of this magic hour between day and night was shattered by horrible screams.

The golden dog didn't hesitate. She ran toward the racket swiftly. It didn't take long for her powerful legs to reach the source of the commotion.

She barreled toward two animals locked in deadly combat, one attacking with knife-sharp teeth, the other hissing and squealing as it attempted to escape. The dog rammed into the swirling ball of fur and began to bark furiously.

The attacker was slender, with a long, narrow body and a thick, impressive tail. He might have seemed cute, a house pet—if he didn't use his teeth like daggers, and if his cries weren't like eerie wails from a

tortured soul. This was a tough customer, bent on tearing apart his prey.

The dog's thunderous presence ended the skirmish. The merciless hunter ran off and vanished into a cluster of trees. The echoes of his human-like cries were left in his wake, like the disturbing memory of a nightmare.

The dog turned to the victim lying on the ground, wheezing with hurt and fear. It was a marmalade cat, whose orange-and-white coat was streaked with blood. Not sure what to do, the dog paced around the wounded cat.

The next thing she knew, she was being pushed aside by a man breathing hard from running. He knelt by the cat, his voice trembling as he offered reassuring words. "Hey there, Butch," he said as he carefully scanned the animal's damaged body. "You had a close call, buddy. It's been a while since I've seen one of those fisher cats around here, and I hope that one learned his lesson."

The cat began to moan. The man straightened up and ran back into the lopsided old farmhouse that was a short walk away. He reemerged a minute later, clutching a blanket, which he wrapped around Butch.

"Doesn't look too bad," he muttered, standing up with Butch in his arms. The man was tall and gaunt, his cheeks sprinkled with gray stubble. His eyes were deeply lined. "Those fishers may be called cats, but they're really just weasels. The only thing they have to do with cats is killing 'em. I'm going to take you to the vet just in case you need a shot."

Then he seemed to remember that the dog was still there. The man glanced down at her.

"What are you waiting around for?" he asked, with a note of amusement in his voice. "A reward?"

The dog didn't really know why she had waited, but something was keeping her there.

Butch meowed in pain.

The man looked at his beloved pet and winced.

The dog remained where she was.

Ignoring her, the man cradled Butch in his arms and carried him toward the house. But as the man stepped onto the porch, he turned and looked back. The dog tilted her head and looked sympathetically at whimpering Butch, who was just a patch of fur sticking up out the blanket the man had wrapped him in.

"Well," said the man slowly as he lifted the cap on his head and put it back on again. "I guess you did send that fisher packing. Stay here."

4

The dog knew what "stay" meant.

So she stayed while the man went inside the house, and she heard him tell someone he was bringing his cat in to be looked at. She remained still, though her stomach rumbled hungrily. Only when the man came back outside with a plate of table scraps did the dog move. She raised her paw in greeting, the way she had been taught by people who had loved her. To her surprise, the man simply stared at the gesture.

"Don't try to get cozy with me, you mutt," he grumbled. "I'm just feeding you something to say thanks for what you did for Butch. Believe me, it's nothing personal."

But his eyes were warm, and when he put the food down by the porch, he gave the dog an awkward pat on the head. Then he dragged over a bucket filled with water and went back inside the house to fetch Butch. Soon the two of them were inside a truck and gone.

After eating, the dog lay down on the grass by the porch and shut her eyes. The sun was sinking and she didn't have anywhere to be.

Her rest didn't last long.

"What do you think you're doing?" someone cackled.

Startled, the dog scrambled to her feet.

"Who are you?" she responded, checking out the copper-colored hen who showed no respect for the dog's superior size and strength.

"*I'm* asking the questions," replied the hen in a haughty voice. "But since you want to know, I'm Penny and I live here."

The dog was amused by the bird's moxie.

"Nice to meet you," she said. "I'm—"

Before she could finish introducing herself, the hen interrupted. "I know who you are," she said. "I saw the whole thing."

Her voice had changed. The dog was pretty sure she heard admiration there.

"You scared off that nasty rascal," Penny said. "That fisher! I know some people feel sorry for him and his kind because they're an endangered species, but try telling that to a housecat. Or a chicken, for that matter. Those weasels are out to get us!"

The dog listened carefully and then answered with a genial bark. "Are you inviting me to hang around?" she asked.

The hen clucked and ran around in a circle. "That's not my place," she said. "That's Mr. Thomas's business, and I've never seen a dog around here. Not till you showed up."

The dog was curious.

"What's Mr. Thomas like?" she asked.

That question put a brake on Penny's skittering. She stopped moving and squatted on the ground, idly pecking at bugs while thinking.

The dog waited patiently until the chicken stopped bobbing her head up and down.

"Oh, yes, Mr. Thomas," Penny said. "Poor thing, he's lived by himself with just that cat too long."

Then the hen's voice was joined by a choir of crickets as they began their screeching serenade. Evening had arrived.

The dog realized she could no longer keep her eyes open. It had been an eventful day. She told Penny it was nice to meet her and then lay down again on the grass next to the porch. The hen walked back to her little yard behind the barn, clucking to herself.

The dog woke up when Mr. Thomas returned with Butch. The cat's neck was wrapped in a large gauze bandage.

"There, there, boy, you aren't hurt too bad," said Mr. Thomas softly as he carried Butch toward the porch. "The vet said you're going to be fine."

The dog was touched by the tenderness she heard in Mr. Thomas's voice. She lifted her head.

"You still here?" Mr. Thomas asked, sounding surprised.

The dog pulled herself to her feet and began wagging her tail.

Mr. Thomas stared at the dog.

"Okay, mutt," he said. "You can stick around. If you drive that weasel away, you'll earn your keep."

The next morning the dog was awakened by Penny.

"You still here?" the hen asked.

"Seems like that's a popular question on this farm," said the dog.

"Hey," said the hen. "You never told me who you are."

The dog paused for a second. "I guess my name is Mutt."

"Mutt!" clucked Penny. "Not much of a name for a hero."

chapter two
MUTT FINDS A FRIEND

M utt kept her bargain with Mr. Thomas. She set out across the large field behind the farmhouse, barking loudly from time to time as a warning to lurking fishers and other unwelcome intruders. As she passed by a patch of woods and a small pond, she memorized her steps, so she would know where to go the next day and the day after, though she wasn't sure how long she would stick around. Since she'd left home, she had been on the move.

She roamed to the far corners of the farm, past orchards where she saw people gathering fruit. The sun warmed her fur. Every so often she paused to take a cooling dip in the creek that ran through the farm. But for most of the day her sense of duty kept her going as surely as the sun moved across the sky.

The day was pleasant and mostly uneventful, except for an encounter with a noisy mob of chickens who didn't realize Mutt was there to protect them. They flapped their wings and squawked mightily until Penny showed up and explained.

"Oh, hello," one or two chickens squawked in Mutt's direction. The rest just went back to scratching the ground and pecking for food as if nothing had happened.

When Mutt returned to the farmhouse, she saw that Butch the cat had emerged to lie on the porch. Before the dog could ask how he was feeling, Butch greeted his rescuer with a yawn and a look that said: "Don't bother me."

Mutt pretended she didn't care. But that evening, after eating the food Mr. Thomas put out for her, she had to admit to herself that she felt a little lonely.

She flopped under a tree and was falling asleep when she heard a small voice call out.

"Hey, Mutt," it said.

Mutt opened one eye, then the other, and then

scrambled to her feet, ready to protect herself.

A boy was standing a few feet away.

"Isn't Mutt your name?" the boy said. "That's what Mr. Thomas called you. I heard him telling someone what you did for that lazy cat of his."

The boy seemed okay. Still, Mutt kept her eyes on the ground.

"I see that you're humble," the boy said with a laugh. "My mother says that's the sign of someone great. You don't need to brag."

The boy didn't move while Mutt walked over to smell him. Satisfied that he was friendly, she sat next to him and allowed him to scratch her behind her ears. It had been a long time since Mutt had had her ears scratched.

"By the way," the boy said formally, sticking out his hand, "my name is Gilberto. But my parents want me to speak English, so in English it's Gilbert."

Finally, Mutt thought, lifting her paw and touching Gilbert's hand, someone around here who has some manners.

"My father and mother work for Mr. Thomas," Gilbert explained.

Then he paused.

"Not exactly for Mr. Thomas," he said. "He used

to own this place, but then he couldn't afford it, so a company bought it from him."

Mutt was interested, but she had enjoyed having her ears scratched so much that she now had a sudden urge to have her belly rubbed. She rolled onto her back.

Gilbert patted the dog's stomach as he kept talking.

"Anyway, they let Mr. Thomas live here and kind of run things, but he's old and doesn't do much," he said. "We just come here to pick fruit. I mean, *I* do until school starts. We'll be here until it turns cold and then we'll move down to Florida for the winter."

Mutt sneezed and Gilbert laughed.

"You probably don't want to know all this," said the boy.

That wasn't true. It was a lot of information to take in, though, and Mutt was tired.

The boy stopped talking and just looked at her, as if he couldn't believe she was there. He reached out and gently touched the fur above her right eye.

"Hey, Mutt," he said, "that white mark on your forehead looks like a crescent moon!"

Mutt had no idea what he was talking about, but she instinctively rolled her eyes toward the spot where Gilbert had placed his finger.

The boy laughed. "Trust me, it's there," he said.

With his finger on the crescent moon above Mutt's eye, Gilbert began to sing: *"Allá está la luna, comiendo aceitunas."*

Mutt joined in with an enthusiastic howl.

The boy burst out laughing.

"You like this silly song my grandmother taught me?" the boy asked. *"Yo le pedí una, no me quiso dar."*

He continued. *"Saqué el pañuelito, me puse a llorar."*

When he stopped, Mutt playfully butted him with her head. She didn't want the evening to end, and was afraid he might leave now that he had stopped singing.

"Oh, you want an encore," the boy said. He began to repeat the song in English.

"There's the moon, eating olives," he began, pretending to put olives in his mouth. "I asked her for one. She didn't want to give me any."

He made sniffling noises. "I took out a tissue. I started to cry."

Mutt whimpered, mimicking the boy.

"You are such a great dog," said the boy, laughing as he hugged her. "I think you understand."

Mutt understood that she felt happy, and that was enough for her.

15

They were interrupted by a voice calling out from beyond the barn.

"Gilbert!"

"Just a minute!" the boy replied.

He ran his finger across the moon above Mutt's eye.

"Gilberto!"

This time Gilbert stood up.

Mutt growled softly. She didn't want him to leave.

"When my mother talks to me in Spanish, she means business!" Gilbert told Mutt. "Good night, my friend." He scratched her head in farewell. "See you tomorrow."

Mutt fell asleep, wondering if the boy who saw the moon in her face was real or a dream.

chapter three

BIG (and Little) CHANGES

Mutt never failed to meet her obligation to Mr. Thomas. After spending much time on the road with nowhere in particular to go, she enjoyed having a schedule. And she liked feeling needed. So every morning, after she had something to eat and the night dew had begun to evaporate, she followed the path she had created.

Yet like many people who are satisfied with their jobs, she couldn't wait for the end of the day. That's when she knew she would see Gilbert. The minute Mutt's work was finished, she would trot across the grass and down the hill to the boy's house. She liked to be there when he returned home from the orchard, his hair matted with sweat, calling her name the instant he spotted her.

Mutt always waited patiently while Gilbert washed in the makeshift shower his father had rigged by the kitchen door. She had discovered that boys and dogs have a lot in common. Both of them could be so tired they couldn't move one minute, and then ready to play the next. After Gilbert cleaned up, they would always run and fling themselves on the ground, over and over, as if they'd spent the day napping. When Gilbert's mother, Silvia, called, they would return to the house and sink onto the grass by the door, ready to eat supper together.

Gilbert's father, Lorenzo, had objected at first. Mutt had listened as he complained to Silvia that he wanted his son with them at the table, not outside with a dog. Silvia's answer came fast and in Spanish. Gilbert had smiled as he translated for Mutt.

"She says she's glad I have a friend," he told the dog. "She says it's her fault that we have to come here to this farm that doesn't have any children, because she couldn't stand to have the family apart every summer with my father working here in Pennsylvania and my mother and me staying in Florida. She says she knows it's lonely for me on the farm, being the only kid."

Mutt understood. Feeling lonely was something

else that she and Gilbert had in common.

The boy and dog peered inside the house as the talking continued that evening. When Silvia fell silent, they could see Lorenzo gazing out at them. A minute later he joined them on the grass, holding a plate in his hand.

"I brought you your dinner," he said, shrugging his shoulders as he gave the plate to Gilbert and tossed a slice of apple toward Mutt.

Gilbert put the plate down and threw his arms around Lorenzo, while Mutt jumped on both of them. Lorenzo laughed and wrapped his arms around both boy and dog.

After that, Mutt had no doubt that she was accepted as part of the family.

They even invited her inside their tiny house. It was more like a cabin, two rooms with the shower outside. But they had added cozy touches. Silvia covered the kitchen table with brightly patterned cloths, and the walls were decorated with family photographs.

One hot day Gilbert whispered to Mutt, "I'm going to show you my secret cave." Mutt felt excited as she watched him look around to make sure no one was watching. Gilbert pressed his fingers to his lips, shushing Mutt as he led her to the back of the house. She watched him drop to all fours and crawl through the opening created by the gap between the house and the earth. Mutt followed his scent as her eyes tried to adjust to the dim light in this cool, shadowy place. The house didn't have a basement, just a dirt foundation. Mutt instantly felt safe and happy there.

At first, Mutt only went to the secret cave with Gilbert. She loved to lie on the damp, soft earth while he told her stories. The temperature was always pleasant, no matter how hot it was outside.

As the summer wore on, she was drawn to the secret cave more often, whether Gilbert came along or not. For the first time in her life, the heat was making her feel sluggish. In fact, she was tired all the time. Yet she never missed a day of work, no matter how exhausted she felt.

Mutt didn't like to complain, but one day she couldn't help herself. She and Gilbert were hanging out together in their cave when she interrupted one of his stories with a loud groan.

Gilbert was alarmed. She had never made a noise like that before.

"What's wrong, girl?" he asked.

Mutt tried to explain the mysterious weight she felt inside, how her belly always felt full even though she could barely eat some days. But all she could do was groan again, even louder than before.

"Wait here," Gilbert said. "I'm going to get my father. He knows a lot about animals."

The worry in Gilbert's voice set off a ripple of fear in Mutt. But she had no choice but to wait while the boy scrambled out of their secret cave and then went inside the house above her. She heard his urgent voice overhead, floating down through the floor.

"Papa," he said, "I think something's wrong with Mutt. Her belly's all swollen and she's making funny noises. Is she sick?"

Hearing the word "sick" made Mutt even more afraid. What was happening to her?

Mutt listened to footsteps again, and then knees cracking as Lorenzo lowered himself onto all fours and began to make his way through the shadows. Gilbert followed right behind him.

"Whew," said Lorenzo, wiping sweat from his forehead, when he reached Mutt.

She tried to lift her paw but she was too weak to be polite.

Lorenzo cleared his throat and patted her on the head.

"I see why you like it down here," he said.

Mutt moaned in discomfort as she felt Lorenzo's gentle hand on her stomach, pressing here and there.

She was surprised to hear him give a little laugh.

"Gilbert," he said, "I think your friend is going to have puppies."

Mutt's surprise turned to shock. Was Lorenzo referring to her? What other friend could he be talking about?

Instead of feeling relieved that she wasn't sick, Mutt was alarmed. Proud and strong as she was, Mutt thought of herself as a youngster, still learning the ways of the world. Now Lorenzo was saying that she, Mutt, was going to become a mother! There were puppies inside her who would expect her to explain things to them the way her mother had explained things to her. How could that be?

Her mind filled with images of her life before she came to Mr. Thomas's farm, as she tried to determine how this moment had arrived. She saw the little girl she had loved as a puppy, and remembered how safe she felt, before she learned the world could be a dangerous place. She sighed, thinking about the father of the puppies. He was a brave dog, too, but he had to follow a different path, determined by the humans he lived with.

She groaned again, not from pain this time but from worry.

"I just won't do it," she said to herself. "I don't know how to do it." She closed her eyes and wished her mother were with her.

Gilbert interrupted her thoughts. "That's amazing!" he said with delight as he hugged her.

Gilbert's mother called from the opening to the outside.

"Lorenzo! Come on, now. We have to go to town."

Lorenzo patted Mutt's belly and put his hand on Gilbert's shoulder.

"*Vámonos,*" he said. "You can see Mutt tonight."

Gilbert looked worried. "Will she be okay?" he asked.

Lorenzo smiled. "You told me she's a hero," he said. "She'll be okay."

Mutt wished she could be as sure as he seemed to be.

23

chapter four

MUTT'S PUPPIES

After Lorenzo and Gilbert left, Mutt lay in the dark trying to comprehend Lorenzo's words. She knew what puppies were and that apparently she was going to have some. But she had no idea what it would mean to be a mother.

Mutt couldn't remember exactly what or how her mother had taught her; they were separated when Mutt was young. But often when she felt lost or uncertain, she heard a voice in her head that was strong and sure, yet tender—her mother's voice. Now Mutt wondered: Would she be able to protect her puppies? Who would show her the way?

These thoughts drifted through her mind over the next few weeks, as her body got heavier and her movements got slower. No matter how awful she felt, she kept her word to Mr. Thomas. Every day, no matter how much she wanted to lie still in Gilbert's secret cave, she patrolled the farm.

One morning, however, she went directly to the crawl space beneath the house. For hours she lay there in the dark, whimpering in pain. She didn't bark, as she usually did, when she heard Gilbert's voice at the end of the day, calling, "Where is Mutt?"

She heard her friend as he ran around the house, repeating her name over and over, but she didn't have the strength to respond. Her entire being was focused on the powerful movements she felt inside of her.

By the time Gilbert scrambled beneath the house to her, Mutt's breathing was coming in short, fast spurts as she paced back and forth, trying to relieve the pressure in her belly. Gilbert reached out his hand to pet her, but Mutt growled at him, the only way she could think of to make him understand that she needed to be alone, that she couldn't focus on anything but the agony she was in.

Mutt lay in the dirt and listened to Gilbert's voice

shaking as he made his way back outside and called, "Mama! Papa!"

She heard Silvia ask, "What's going on?" And she heard Gilbert describe what he'd seen and heard and then blurt out, "I think Mutt is dying!"

Mutt hurt so badly she almost wished it were true. Then she heard Lorenzo speak.

"Mutt isn't dying," he said to Gilbert. "I think those puppies are ready to come out."

Mutt shuddered in pain as Gilbert cried out, "Can't we do anything to help?!" Mutt strained to listen to what Silvia had to say. She was female like Mutt, and had given birth.

"Mutt is strong," Silvia said. "She's probably scared, but she's in a nice dark place where she can feel safe. Her body knows what to do. Now we just have to wait."

While the humans waited, Mutt directed her courage and determination to the bewildering task of pushing the puppies out of her. It was a noisy and painful business, but finally a tiny being emerged, wet and helpless. Without thinking, Mutt bit the cord connecting her to the puppy and began to lick the wriggling creature clean.

That's when it hit her. *She was a mother and this was her baby.*

There was no time for sentimentality, however. Her belly was still full of puppies. For the next several hours, she waited until it was time to push another one out. Somehow she knew what she had to do. One by one, these strange little creatures emerged until there were four of them, three females and one male. One by one, Mutt greeted them by biting the cord that connected them and licking them clean. Only then did she rest, her new family nestled against her.

Shortly after dawn, she was wakened by weird high-pitched noises. Could there be bats in their cave, even though it wasn't really a cave? Had the fisher cat returned? Tired as she was, Mutt's body came alive, ready to strike back if someone attacked.

Then she realized the sounds were coming from the puppies. *Her* puppies. She relaxed and gave them

each an affectionate lick. To the outsider, they might seem like shivering, screaming blobs of fur, aliens huddling together for warmth, not yet able to see or hear. But to their mother, they were miniature Mutts in the making,

Mutt glanced at the tiny bodies next to her, satisfied with her night's work. Then she sighed and fell back to sleep, already unable to remember what it was like when the puppies weren't there.

chapter five

WHAT'S IN A NAME?

While human babies could take a year or more to learn how to stand, Mutt's puppies were up on their wobbly little legs before a month had gone by. Soon they were running around, crashing into one another gleefully, and then getting up to run some more.

They thought Gilbert was one of them. With their new teeth, they grabbed the scraps of cloth he brought them, wrestling one another for control of the tiniest piece. When the boy sang his song about the moon eating olives, the puppies joined in with their high-pitched yaps while Mutt watched.

One evening Gilbert tried a new game with the puppies. He threw himself on the ground and rolled down the small hill by his house, while the puppies raced to keep up. The boy tumbled faster and faster—until he was stopped by a large work boot. It was attached to Mr. Thomas.

The puppies kept on playing—all except for one, the smallest of the bunch, one of the females.

This puppy was a worrier. She watched intently as Gilbert sat on the ground, wiping blades of grass off his shirt.

"Hello, Mr. Thomas," Gilbert muttered.

Mr. Thomas reached out his hand to help Gilbert to his feet.

"I hear you've been a big help to Mutt with her pups," the man said. Though the man was much bigger than Gilbert, his voice was soft.

Gilbert simply nodded.

The curious little puppy kept listening.

"How old are they now?" Mr. Thomas asked.

Gilbert finally spoke. "About six weeks," he said. Adding: "Sir."

"How many are there?" Mr. Thomas asked.

Looking down at his sneakers, Gilbert responded. "Four," he said.

He added, "It's a small litter for a big dog, but that's not strange for the first time."

Mr. Thomas smiled. "How do you know so much?" he asked.

Gilbert looked up. "My father told me."

Then Mr. Thomas asked a question that made the puppy's ears perk up.

"You named them yet?" he asked.

Gilbert was flustered. "Yes, no, sort of," he stammered.

Mr. Thomas grunted. "Well, which is it, yes, no, or maybe?"

Gilbert shrugged.

"I wanted to tell you I've noticed what a good friend you've been to Mutt," the farmer said in a quiet voice. "And to her puppies," he added.

Gilbert's face brightened. "Thanks," he said.

Mr. Thomas nodded and then stretched his arms behind his back. "Whew," he said, "I'm creaking a little."

Gilbert said politely, "I'm sorry."

Mr. Thomas stared down at the boy with a wistful smile. "How old are you now?" he asked.

Gilbert looked startled. "Ten," he said.

"You in school?" Mr. Thomas asked, as though they were meeting for the first time.

Gilbert nodded.

"That's good," Mr. Thomas said. "Very good. Your father is a good man."

He and Gilbert stood in uncomfortable silence.

"Do you want to talk to my parents?" Gilbert asked.

Mr. Thomas pulled his cap off and wiped the sweat from his forehead.

"Nope," he said, shaking his head. "You're the one I wanted to talk to. To say thank you. That's done now."

Then the man smiled and waved awkwardly as he walked away.

When he left, Gilbert knelt next to the puppy, who hadn't moved.

"Until today, Mr. Thomas hasn't said more than three words to me," the boy said. "Weird, huh?"

The puppy agreed and let Gilbert know by butting his hand with her head. The other puppies took this as a signal to tumble. Soon they were all bouncing off Gilbert as if the boy were a trampoline. When they were tired out, they collapsed next to him.

They listened as he began to talk.

"I think it's time for you to have names," he said in a formal voice. "My name in Spanish means 'bright promise.' Every year on my birthday my mother tells me how I got my name. She says, 'Your father and I thought we would never have a child. We tried and tried but nothing happened . . . until you. You are our child of destiny.'"

The littlest puppy sighed. "That's beautiful," she whispered.

Her brother, the biggest of the bunch, teased her. "Is that what you think you are?" he asked. "A child of destiny?"

Before she could reply, Gilbert picked up the male puppy and stared at him.

"Let's see," he said. "What is unique about you?"

Gilbert looked very serious as he held the chubby brown puppy up in the air.

"The others always follow you, big fellow," he said. "I'm going to call you *Jefe,* Chief, because I can see you are going to be very strong."

When Gilbert placed Chief gently on the ground, his little sister saw the pride in his eyes. She was excited, wondering what Gilbert would say about *her.*

But she would have to wait. One of her bigger sisters ran up to Gilbert and nuzzled his foot.

She was beige with dark fur around her eyes and was always ready to play.

Gilbert didn't hesitate.

"You are definitely Alegre," he said. "That's Spanish for 'happy.'"

The little puppy started to walk toward the boy and was knocked aside by her other sister, who looked just like Alegre. Annoyed, the little puppy watched this sister nuzzle Gilbert's other foot.

She was even more annoyed when the boy laughed!

"Okay," he said. "I'm just going to call you Happy. That way, if I mix the two of you up, it won't matter. Your names mean the same thing!"

Only the littlest puppy was left. Her heart skipped when he finally turned to her.

Gilbert knelt next to her and said something that surprised her, but made her happy.

"You look the most like Mutt," the boy said in a gentle voice. "I've watched you, little one, always right next to your mama. I think you aren't just the smallest, you are the shyest."

The puppy's ears perked up. He understood her!

She tried to tell him how glad she was, but he didn't seem to understand what she was saying.

"Are you singing?" Gilbert asked.

He pulled her to his chest and rubbed his finger on her tiny head.

"Look!" he said. "You have the same mark as Mutt!

"Of course," said Gilbert softly, holding the puppy close to him. "You are Luna, the child of the moon."

He began to sing the song about the moon and the olives.

Luna wiggled in his hands.

Gilbert laughed.

"You must love that song," he said. "You are danc-ing to the music."

Luna giggled. She wasn't dancing, exactly. She had to pee—and she did, all over Gilbert's hands.

"Luna!" he exclaimed. "That's why you were wig-gling? Gross! Is that how you thank me for giving you such a beautiful name?"

Luna scampered over to her mother, who had been there all the time, watching. Mutt bent her head to nuzzle her little one.

Gilbert leaned down and rubbed his hands in the grass. When they were dry, he knelt by Mutt and scratched her head.

Then he lifted Luna again and began to move her back and forth through the air. The puppy waved her paws in excitement as the air swept across her fur. She felt free and unafraid, as if she could do any-thing, go anywhere.

When he put her back on the ground, Luna kept moving, one paw after the other.

"Hey Luna," Gilbert said. "Look at you, dancing on your own! You can dance all the way to the moon."

Luna didn't know how far away the moon was, but she loved to dance so much, she would be willing to try.

chapter six

PUPPY DAYS

After the thrill of her first dance, Luna scampered to the comfort of her mother's warm belly. She snuggled there, watching the boy until he disappeared. She yawned with contentment, remembering his sunbaked human smell as he lifted her into the warm summer air.

The peaceful moment was soon disrupted as her brother and sisters piled around her. She grunted from under the crush of furry bodies.

Teeth gripped the skin on her neck and plucked her out of the crowd.

"C'mon, Luna," said her big brother, the bruiser Gilbert had named Chief. "Stand up for yourself."

Luna blinked her eyes, wondering for a second who he was talking to.

Mutt's deep voice chimed in.

"You are my daydreamer," she said, licking dirt off her smallest baby's head.

Luna watched as Mutt looked at Chief.

"You are the biggest and the strongest," Mutt said. "You look like your father, but you are steady like me. I won't be able to take care of you pups forever. I'll be counting on you, Chief, to watch over the rest, especially Luna."

Chief responded by rolling on his back, and brought Luna along for the ride, her scruff clamped in his teeth. Not wanting to miss the fun, the other pups jumped in.

From the pile of fur and ears and tails, Chief called out, panting from exertion, "Don't worry, Mother. I'll watch out for Luna."

"And one day *she* will do the same for *you*," Luna was pleased to hear her mother say. "Strength is like a seesaw; sometimes up and sometimes down."

Luna wasn't sure what a "seesaw" was, but she

understood what Mutt meant, though she couldn't imagine what she could do for Chief. He was so big and she was so small.

Day by day Luna and her siblings ventured farther away from their patch of the farm, the area surrounding the house where Gilbert's family stayed. The two Happys—Happy and Alegre—usually led the pack. Carefree types, they were the first to run across the gravel road that led to the fields, and up to the entrance into the barn across the way. Chief was close behind, barking at them to slow down.

"I'm the chief," he panted.

Happy and Alegre just laughed at him as they ran even faster.

Luna got frustrated with them because she couldn't help herself from stopping every so often to dance and dream.

Then she would call out, "Wait for me!"

But she didn't panic too much. She knew that if she trailed too far behind, Chief would circle back to bring her along.

Together and separately, she and the others discovered the ways of their little patch of the world.

Every smell, every crack in the earth, was an invitation to adventure. The puppies kept their noses stuck to the ground as they dashed about, inhaling the fragrance of hay, poking their heads into the inviting spaces provided by parked tractors and plows. Life was one surprise after another.

It didn't take them long, however, to learn that not every creature was delighted by their presence.

The revelation came the day Alegre and Happy led the pack inside the barn, with Luna panting to catch up. When her sisters reached the other side of the barn, Luna watched as they almost ran over a bunch of tiny creatures bouncing around like little yellow balls.

"Watch where you're going!" squeaked one of the balls.

Before the puppies could retort, they were startled by a fierce noise.

"Get out of here!" clucked a giant hen, screaming at them as she spread her dark reddish brown feathers into a menacing pose. Luna was terrified. She had never seen anything like this, but she understood immediately that this crazy creature could be dangerous.

She and the other puppies scattered, madly jostling to get out of the barn, across the gravel road, and

back home. Luna watched as Chief and the others dived under Gilbert's house like a squadron of tiny jets back from a dangerous mission and disappeared!

Her heart started to beat very fast. Then, without realizing what she was doing, she began to skip backward and forward.

Soon she heard someone barking, "Luna! Luna!"

It was Chief.

"What are you doing?" he asked her.

She stopped and rubbed her head against her brother's neck.

"You guys all disappeared and I was scared," she said. "So I started dancing to calm myself down."

Chief sighed.

"C'mon," he said.

Luna bounced alongside her big brother.

They ran up to Mutt to find their sisters were still yelping about their adventure.

"You should have seen this giant thing," Happy said.

". . . that chased us and yelled at us," said Alegre, finishing her sister's sentence.

"It wasn't all that big," Chief said as he sat down next to his sisters. "Just weird and very, very noisy."

He lowered his head onto his paws and yawned.

"They're wimps," he said, looking at his sisters.

Happy and Alegre began to object in unison.

Mutt laughed.

"Calm down, all of you," she said. "That weird, noisy thing was Penny the hen."

"You know her?" Chief asked.

"I do," said Mutt. "She was my first acquaintance here on the farm. Those little yellow things are her chicks."

Luna whispered, "What are chicks?"

Chief piped up. "Those are baby birds," he said, "like we're baby dogs."

Luna sighed. "How do you know so much, Chief?"

He scratched the ground with his paw. "I pay attention," he said. "I have to. I'm the oldest."

Luna and her sisters piled on top of him.

"Oldest!" Alegre barked. "Just because you came out first?"

Mutt spoke up. "That's right," she said. "Just because he came out first."

She smiled at her biggest, oldest puppy.

Happy asked, "Why did that old bird have to be so mean? We weren't doing any harm."

Mutt replied, "She's watching out for her chicks the way I'm watching out for you."

"Guess we are pretty scary to those chicks," Chief said, looking pleased.

Luna giggled at the thought of seeming scary to anyone.

"Let's go chase a chick" became the puppies' rallying cry, though they always stopped shy of the area where Penny marched around her flock of chirping babes.

Luna began to keep up with the rest. She would never forget those early days when nothing was ordinary and the smallest adventure seemed grand.

chapter seven

MUTT'S PROMISE

Gilbert tried not to play favorites, but he loved Luna best.

He didn't say it, but Luna knew.

Often when the other puppies roamed, she was content to hang out with the boy. When he began to teach her tricks, she learned quickly because she was eager to please him.

Soon, when Gilbert commanded, "Dance, Luna," and sang the words to the song about the moon and olives, she knew she was supposed to kick with her right leg, then the left, and then turn all the way around. Then he just had to hum the tune and nod—and Luna would dance.

When he ordered her to run, she ran. When he told her to sit, she sat. Without needing an explanation, she understood that he believed she was special.

One day when Luna finished her dance, Gilbert didn't clap the way he usually did.

"You have to bow at the end," he said to her.

Luna cocked her head, which was her way to say that she didn't understand.

"Like this," Gilbert said as he raised one hand in the air and lowered his head.

Luna didn't get it. When Gilbert bowed, she ran over and tried to jump up and lick his face.

"I know this may seem silly to you," Gilbert said, "but the bow is your way of saying 'you are welcome' when the crowd applauds." Luna didn't know why he sounded frustrated.

Next time she danced for him, he clapped and said, "Bow."

Luna just looked at him. She didn't understand.

The time after that, Gilbert pushed down on Luna's head after he clapped, and said, "Bow."

She thought he was playing a game and flopped over

on her back, but he just sighed instead of petting her.

The next time Luna finished dancing, Gilbert surprised her by dropping a cracker on the ground. But when she bent over to grab it in her teeth, he snatched it away before she got to it.

"Not yet," he said.

Slipping the cracker into his pocket, he told her to dance. When she was finished, he told her to sit, and then he dropped the cracker on the ground again.

When she started to run for it, he commanded her to stay. Though she was puzzled, she stayed, waiting to see what would happen next.

Gilbert began to clap his hands.

"Okay," he said.

Luna slowly walked over to the cracker and bent her head to reach it. This time Gilbert didn't stop her.

"Good bow, Luna!" he said.

Now she understood what he wanted! After that, when she heard the sound of clapping, she gave a little bow, whether there was a cracker there or not.

She was pleased to see how delighted Gilbert was. She loved it when he said, "You are so smart!" She was happy when he began to confide in her, the way he confided in Mutt.

He told Luna how hard it was when his dad used to live apart from them for months at a stretch. "He worked for people who treated him worse than a dog," he said. "Not like Mr. Thomas."

Luna put her head on the ground and covered her eyes with her paws at the sound of that.

"Whoops, sorry," Gilbert said. "I meant worse than the way some *crazy* people treat dogs."

Luna whimpered.

Gilbert continued. "My dad did such a good job here that Mr. Thomas made him foreman and let him bring us with him for the picking season. That was good, but hard, because every year I start school here and then have to leave after a couple of months, when we move south for the winter crops and I have to start another school."

He told Luna about his father's dream, to open a restaurant with Gilbert's uncle, who lived in a big city.

Luna didn't always get what Gilbert was saying, but sometimes the most important part of being a friend is knowing when to just listen. And Luna knew how to listen.

When she was around Gilbert, she felt as though she could do anything. But she hadn't shaken off her shyness. When she was out roaming with the other puppies, she stuck to Chief like a gnat.

Often she preferred to stay by her mother's side.

"Why didn't you go with the rest?" Mutt asked her one afternoon.

Luna lowered her head.

"They were heading over to the big house and I was scared," she said.

Mutt lifted her paw and laid it gently on Luna's small back.

"What were you scared of?" she asked.

Luna shrugged and then offered a list.

"Of Mr. Thomas, of the tractor, of thunder, of cows, of worms—"

Her mother laughed. "Of worms?"

It was true. Luna had jumped in terror when a worm crawled on her paw the other day.

Luna nodded and continued. "Of not seeing Gilbert again—"

Mutt interrupted again.

"Why are you worried about that?" Mutt asked.

"I don't know, but I am," Luna replied. "And Mama, what if I have to go away from you? I won't know what to do."

Mutt gazed at Luna for a while, then said, "When I was your age, I was afraid like you."

Luna looked at her mother.

"I don't believe you were ever afraid of anything!" she said.

Mutt licked her baby pup.

"Oh, I was afraid of many things," she said.

A strange look came across Mutt's face. "I just remembered something," she said. "My mother used to scold me for being a scaredy-cat."

Luna giggled. "That's so silly!" she said.

Mutt smiled.

"I *was* a bit of a scaredy-cat," she said. "Mainly because I didn't know much, and when you don't know what things are, they can seem frightening."

Luna nodded. She understood exactly what Mutt was saying.

"But that changed," Mutt said tenderly. "I found something I was good at and I became less afraid."

Luna listened carefully.

"As you know, I'm an excellent watchdog," Mutt said, not bragging but simply stating a fact. "That's my talent. And one day you will find yours. I promise you that."

Luna curled up into a ball.

"I could never be like you," she whimpered.

Mutt lowered her head to touch Luna's.

"You are more like me than you know," she said. "Now, go out and play! It's a beautiful day."

chapter eight

THE END OF SUMMER

Luna sensed that changes were coming, and it wasn't just because the days were shorter and nights were cooler. Mutt seemed to be testing the puppies. Now when they went swimming in the pond, instead of watching them from under the big tree, she headed back to the house. Sometimes when she rested in the crawl space where they were born, she barked until they ran away instead of lifting her paw in welcome the way she had before.

Luna saw that Gilbert noticed too.

"Mutt, stop barking," he yelled at her when she

let loose a barrage of noise, aimed at her puppies. "What's wrong with you?"

Luna watched as Mutt walked over to Gilbert and sat down next to him, raising her paw.

"I don't get it," the boy said, kneeling down and shaking her uplifted paw. "For weeks you barely look at me because of the puppies, and now you want to be my friend again but you push away the pups."

Mutt whimpered and laid her head on Gilbert's lap.

He scratched her ears and said with exasperation, "Dogs!"

When Gilbert left, Luna tiptoed up to her mother. Before Mutt could growl, Luna dived next to her.

Mutt started to push the puppy away and then sighed as she allowed Luna to snuggle next to her.

"What's going on, Mama?" Luna asked.

Mutt gently nuzzled Luna and then she explained.

"Dogs understand what people find hard to accept," she said, "that we can create new life but we can't own it forever."

Luna felt frightened.

"What do you mean?" she asked.

Mutt licked Luna's face gently.

"I am proud of you, Chief, and your sisters," she

said. "You are stronger every day. Now what happens to you depends on you—and on fate."

Luna was confused.

"Okay, but why do you have to be mean to us?" she asked.

Mutt smiled. "I'm not being mean," she said. "I'm just making sure you learn to take care of yourself."

Luna cocked her head and started to say something. But Mutt stopped her with a frisky head bump.

"Now go play while you can," Mutt said. "Winter will be here soon enough."

Luna scampered away and almost ran into Gilbert and his father. They were in the middle of an intense discussion.

Gilbert picked up Luna and stroked her ears as he continued talking to Lorenzo.

"Papa, what are you saying?" Gilbert asked. "Won't the puppies be here when we come back next year?"

Lorenzo didn't answer right away.

"Gilbert, a lot can happen in a year," he finally said mysteriously. "Who knows where we will be? Maybe our plans will change."

Luna's ears lifted. *What is going on?* she wondered. *First Mother is talking about winter coming and now Gil-*

56

bert's father is saying he doesn't know where they will be?

Gilbert seemed as confused as she was. "What do you mean?" he asked. "I want to come back here. I don't even want to leave!"

His words made Luna growl.

Lorenzo smiled. "This is a different song than the one you usually sing," he said. "Every year you can't wait to get out of here and be with your cousins in Florida. Every year you say you hate starting school here and then having to switch."

Gilbert burst into tears. "That was before I met Mutt," he said. "And Luna! What would she do without me?"

Luna pressed her body tight against Gilbert, as if she were trying to glue him to her so he couldn't go away. Gilbert hugged her until she yelped.

Lorenzo was about to say something but was interrupted by the other puppies. They had come back to find Luna, and now that they saw her in Gilbert's arms, they wanted his attention too.

As Chief, Happy, and Alegre raced around them, Gilbert kept his hold on Luna.

"Hey Luna," Gilbert whispered. "When I'm gone and you see the moon, think of me and the song about olives. And don't forget the tricks I taught you. I'll test you when I see you next time!"

For the first time in her life, Luna understood what sadness meant. The air felt heavy as she watched Lorenzo put his arm around Gilbert and as she heard Gilbert's words.

"Wherever I am," he said to her, "I'll watch for the moon and think of you, waiting for me to come back next summer."

She licked his face and he laughed.

"Okay," he said. "Sealed with a kiss."

For the next few days, Luna barely left Gilbert's side. She was there on his last day at the farm when Mr. Thomas walked down to Gilbert's cabin to say good-bye. The door was open. Gilbert and Luna watched as the farmer gazed around the cabin, where all the little touches that made the cabin a home were gone—the curtains Gilbert's mother had hung, the photographs, the pots she used for cooking.

Luna barked, to let Mr. Thomas know they were there.

The farmer said awkwardly to Gilbert, "That one is Luna."

Gilbert nodded. Luna was surprised that the farmer

knew her name. He never seemed to pay attention to her and her siblings.

As if he read her thoughts, Mr. Thomas said, "I remembered she was the one with the mark over her eye.

"Like Mutt," the man added.

He stood there stiffly and then said to Gilbert, "I've gotten a kick out of watching you and those puppies."

Gilbert looked at the man and smiled.

He said, "Luna, dance for Mr. Thomas."

Hesitating, Luna lowered her head.

"For me?" Gilbert asked.

Luna looked back and forth between the man and boy and wished she could tell Mr. Thomas to make Gilbert's family stay. Then, without thinking, she was up on her feet and they were moving all on their own. As long as she was dancing, she couldn't feel sad. As long as she was dancing, she felt that she would find her way, just as Mutt had promised.

When she finished, Mr. Thomas clapped and Luna bowed.

Mr. Thomas reached over and patted her head.

"Good dog," he said.

"Gilbert!"

At the sound of his mother's voice, Gilbert said in a sad voice, "I have to go."

Luna couldn't believe her ears. Gilbert was actually leaving! She was in a daze as she felt Gilbert hug her and heard him say good-bye, his voice shaking with sobs. The next thing she knew, she was standing in the driveway with Mr. Thomas and Mutt as they watched Gilbert, Lorenzo, and Silvia climb into a truck packed with their things. When the truck backed onto the road, Luna saw Mr. Thomas raise his hand. She felt Mutt's nose touch her head and then saw her mother's paw lift in farewell.

Luna didn't want to say good-bye.

Don't leave, she thought as she reluctantly lifted her paw.

A few seconds later, as if her wish had been granted, the truck reappeared in the driveway.

Luna's heart leaped. Maybe they had changed their minds!

"Wonder what they forgot," Mr. Thomas muttered.

The back door opened and Gilbert jumped out. He ran over to Mutt and Luna and held his hand out to one, then the other.

"I saw you lift your paws and didn't want to leave

without shaking hands," he said. "I didn't want to leave without saying I love you."

He gave each of them a hug, even Mr. Thomas, and then gathered Luna in his arms one last time.

"Don't forget how to dance, Luna," Gilbert cried out as he ran back to the truck. "Don't forget me!"

As the family drove away, Luna forced herself to move her feet, three steps forward, three steps back, her way of promising her friend that she would never forget him.

chapter nine

SIGNS OF CHANGE

utumn had arrived. As nights grew colder, the puppies and Mutt began to sleep in the barn, finding warmth among the hay bales. They went up to the farmhouse once a day, to eat the food Mr. Thomas put out for them in large bowls. Sometimes Luna saw him watching them from behind the screen door.

From time to time she stopped by Gilbert's cabin, hoping he might show up—but he never did.

Luna was becoming more self-sufficient every day. Though she missed her friend, she didn't mope. She joined Chief and their sisters as they made their rounds. She barked at chicks and dipped her paws in the pond full of muck. She practiced her dance steps, always ready for the moment Gilbert would reappear.

Meanwhile, they all noticed that Mr. Thomas had changed for the better. Penny the chicken remarked that he was happier than she could remember.

"How can you tell?" Luna asked.

"Haven't you noticed?" Penny said. "He still spends most of his time indoors with Butch, just as he always did. But he must spend a lot of time fixing dinner for you puppies and your mom."

Mutt answered. "That's true," she said. "We've been getting more variety than we used to."

Luna chimed in. "It's just his leftovers, Mom," she said.

Mutt shook her head. "But he cooks it, and there's definitely more meat and vegetables than there used to be."

Luna nodded. "You have a point," she said. "And even old Butch has stopped hissing at me and the other puppies when we come by."

The days continued to pass pleasantly enough until Mr. Thomas received a letter that changed everything. It was so upsetting that he read it to himself and then read it all over again out loud to Butch, who felt the need to tell Mutt about it, right in front of the puppies.

"Here's what the letter said," the cat reported, repeating what he'd heard almost word for word.

Dear Mr. Thomas,

I hope you are well. I am writing to thank you for giving me a chance to prove myself. Before I came to your place, I had worked for many people who treated me and other workers worse than their animals. You were not like that. So I wanted to let you know that I and my family will not be returning to your orchards. I have saved enough money to do what I have dreamed about. I have joined my brother in New York City and we are opening a small restaurant, together with my wife. We have a location picked out on Broadway—not the one in Manhattan but the one in Brooklyn. I just wanted to let you know in case you wondered where we were, and to give you time to get another foreman before the season begins.

Sincerely,
Lorenzo

P.S. Gilbert made me promise to thank you for watching the dogs for him. As you can imagine, he will miss them very much.

Luna couldn't believe what she was hearing.

"What is he saying, Mama?" Luna asked Mutt. "Isn't Gilbert coming back?"

Mutt shook her head. "I don't think so," she said sadly.

Luna's whole body drooped, and when Chief came over to cheer her up, she put her head down.

"We should feel happy for Lorenzo," Mutt said, though her voice betrayed her disappointment.

Luna sat up. "What did Mr. Thomas say about it?" she asked Butch.

The cat stretched from the tip of his paws to the end of his tail.

"Well, naturally he was upset," he said. "He crumpled up the letter and tossed it on the floor and said something like, 'A restaurant! Good luck with that!'"

Luna realized this was the longest conversation they'd ever had with Butch, who usually kept his distance. It occurred to her that the lazy old cat loved Mr. Thomas and was upset on his behalf. Butch said he sensed that Mr. Thomas admired Lorenzo's willingness to pursue his dreams.

Luna must have shown her surprise, because Butch kept on talking. "You don't know it, but Mr. Thomas gave up on his dreams long ago." The cat sighed.

"Not that he could say any of that out loud. No, all he said about Lorenzo's letter was that he wouldn't enjoy looking for a new foreman."

After that, Luna took a new interest in Mr. Thomas. She soon noticed that he had changed again—and not for the better. Now when the puppies came running toward the house for their supper, the farmer no longer gave them a pat on the head or said hello; he just put their food down. They overheard him grumbling about how much they were costing him and even heard him imagining out loud that soon they would be large dogs, needing more and more food and attention.

"Why is Mr. Thomas so grumpy?" Luna asked her mother.

"Disappointment can become like a hungry, living thing," Mutt said. "It starts eating away at your ability to feel happiness or even think straight and can get so big, it blocks out every other feeling you might have."

She looked worried. "I hope that isn't happening to Mr. Thomas," she said, more to herself than to Luna.

Worry could eat at you the same as disappointment, Luna discovered. After hearing her mother's words, the puppy made it her business to keep an even closer eye on Mr. Thomas. She was watching on the morning he showed up on the porch with a large piece of wood and some paint. Without acknowledging Luna, Mr. Thomas carefully dipped a brush into the paint and applied it to the wood. Then he nailed the wood to a stake and carried the whole thing to the side of the road, the same road that had taken Gilbert away from Luna.

She watched as he pounded the stake into the ground and then stood back and admired the sign he had made. She listened as he read what he'd painted:

FREE PUPPIES
ASK ME ABOUT IT
JUST KNOCK ON THE DOOR

No sooner had the words left his mouth than a loud noise caused him (and Luna) to jump.

It was Penny the hen, squawking loudly in disapproval.

"I may not want those puppies around my chicks," she scolded, "but you have plenty of room on the farm. Why do you have to give them away?"

Mr. Thomas couldn't understand her, but Luna stood frozen in horror as Penny's words began to sink in. She heard Mr. Thomas mutter to himself, "I was

only keeping those puppies for the boy. Now there isn't anyone to take care of them. Old Mutt is almost more than I can handle."

Penny squawked again. "Gilbert took care of Mutt almost since the day she got here," she cackled. "And because of Mutt the fisher cats haven't been back. Some bargain you made!"

Mr. Thomas kept right on talking to himself, as if Penny weren't there.

"I'll make sure they go someplace good to live," he told himself. "Someone will be happy to take them."

That's all Luna needed to hear. She raced down to the barn to find her family and tell them what was going on.

But only Mutt seemed to share her alarm.

Chief always stayed calm, and Happy and Alegre were actually enthusiastic about the prospect of living somewhere else. They immediately began to chatter about who might adopt them, pausing only to run over and lick Mutt and tell her how much they loved her.

"It isn't that we want to leave you, Mother," said Happy.

"It's just so exciting to imagine where we might go," added Alegre.

Chief interrupted. "What makes you think it will be 'we'?" he asked. "What if you get separated?"

The two of them dismissed the thought with a giggle and ran off.

When Luna looked at Mutt with a question in her eyes, Mutt gently sat down next to her and said, "We'll just have to wait and see."

They didn't have to wait long. Within a day, a little girl arrived at the farm with her parents. She spotted Happy and Alegre right away.

"They're identical twins!" she exclaimed.

The two puppies responded to the glee in her voice by showing off all their tricks. Happy bounded over Alegre, who rolled on her back waving her feet in the air.

The girl didn't seem to notice Luna and Chief, who were there too.

"Can you believe this?" Luna asked Chief. Then she added grumpily, "They aren't really identical. Happy has a white circle around her left eye and Alegre's is around her right."

"They are twin clowns," Chief said with a sniff. "They'll do anything for attention. It's undignified, the way they never stop bouncing around. They might as well scream it out: 'Look at me! Look at me!'"

71

Luna worked up her courage to contradict the brother she adored.

"I think they're really funny," she confessed. Then she added, under her breath, "I wish I could be more like them."

"Shh," said Chief, perking up his ears. "Let's see what's going on."

Mr. Thomas had come outside to greet the visitors.

"Sorry, folks," he said. "They just get excited when people stop by."

The little girl's mother laughed.

"We don't mind," she said. "Lisa hasn't stopped nagging us to come out here since we passed your sign. We promised her we'd get her a puppy, so here we are."

Mr. Thomas nodded slowly.

"You folks aren't from around here?" he asked.

The mother replied, "I grew up here, but we're just visiting."

Mr. Thomas nodded again. He didn't have much practice talking to strangers.

Lisa was down on the ground rolling on her back like she was another puppy. Happy and Alegre jumped on top of her while the others kept a slight distance.

Luna and Chief watched as the girl jumped to her feet and motioned for her obviously adoring parents to lean down so she could whisper in their ears.

"Oh, I don't know about that," her father said.

"Honey, that isn't what we'd discussed," said her mother.

Lisa talked some more in a low voice.

Then her mother and father talked to each other in whispers.

Lisa's father knelt down to pet Happy and Alegre, who responded by nuzzling his hand.

Chief watched with a thoughtful look on his face.

"You have to give those two credit," he said to Luna. "They know how to get their way."

Lisa's parents excused themselves and stood to one side, whispering and glancing over at the puppies.

"We'll take two puppies," the father said. The words were barely out of his mouth when Lisa almost knocked him over, she was so excited.

Lisa's father put out his hand for Mr. Thomas to shake.

"These two," he said, pointing at Happy and Alegre. Luna didn't want to leave her mother, but she felt a pang of disappointment at not being chosen.

"Do they have names?" Lisa asked.

Mr. Thomas put his hand on the baseball cap he always wore, a sign he was thinking.

"You know," he said, "the Mexican boy who works here summers told me . . ."

Luna had to hold back a tear.

The girl looked interested. "Where is he?" she said. "How old is he? What's his name?"

"He and his family went back to Florida," said Mr. Thomas. "They just work here for fruit season. Let's see, how old is he?"

"He's ten," Luna whispered to Chief. "Gilbert told him! I was there."

Mr. Thomas remembered.

"Ten," he said, looking at Lisa. "Maybe a little older than you."

He fell silent.

Lisa prompted him.

"His name?"

As Mr. Thomas smiled, Luna remembered the warmth of summer and the happiness she had felt when her friend was there.

"Gilbert," he said. "He's a bright boy. Gilbert."

The girl asked, "What about the puppies?"

"What *about* the puppies?" Mr. Thomas repeated.

"Their names?" Lisa reminded him.

"Right," the farmer said, and looked like he was concentrating.

"One of them is Happy . . ." he began.

"Happy!" shrieked Lisa. "I love that."

"And I sort of think the other one has the same name, but in Spanish," said Mr. Thomas.

"Alegre!" shouted Lisa.

Her father looked at his daughter with surprise and pride.

"How did you know that?" he asked.

"Daaaad," she said. "We learned that in school. *Alegre,* happy. *Triste,* sad."

Mr. Thomas cleared his throat. "Smart girl you got there," he said.

Mr. Thomas looked down at Luna and Chief.

"You sure you don't want these two as well?" he asked. "They're good dogs too, just like their mother."

Luna held her breath, not knowing what she wanted the answer to be.

She wasn't in suspense more than a second. A look of alarm came across the father's face.

"Two dogs is more than enough!" he said, then laughed.

Mr. Thomas didn't ask again.

For the first time Luna could remember, Happy and Alegre looked sad.

"We'll miss you," each of them said as they walked over to Chief, Luna, and Mutt to lick their faces farewell. A few minutes later Happy and Alegre were gone, vanished just like Gilbert and his family.

chapter ten
A STRANGER ARRIVES

Mutt would never forget the instant she saw Raymond, a tense, slender man with icy eyes. He appeared in the barn with Mr. Thomas one bone-chilling morning, just before winter. Raymond was pulling a wagon behind him, carrying some kind of contraption.

Mutt had never seen a cage before but she would soon learn what it was, all too well.

As the men approached Luna and Chief, Mutt began growling fiercely.

"What's wrong, Mutt?" Mr. Thomas asked with surprise in his voice. "Raymond saw our sign and wants to find Chief and Luna new homes with people who can take care of them. He owns a puppy farm that has contacts in the city. Chief and Luna will be with other puppies in a great place until Raymond finds them the right homes."

The words didn't matter to Mutt. Raymond had put her instincts on high alert, as surely as if he were a fisher cat. She couldn't stop growling.

"Mutt, stop that!" Mr. Thomas scolded. "What's gotten into you? Quiet down."

Mutt tried to obey her master but she couldn't stop herself. The hair on her back went up and she began to bark furiously.

The puppies, who had never seen her in this kind of frightened fury, joined her in a chorus of deafening barks.

Mr. Thomas looked alarmed.

"I'm sorry," he said. "I don't know what's got into them. They usually are a friendly bunch."

"Don't worry about it," Raymond said with a deep chuckle.

Mutt found that low laugh more nerve-wracking than a shout would have been. Mr. Thomas must have felt the same way. His lips were pressed tightly together.

"Don't worry, Mr. Thomas," repeated Raymond,

staring at the three dogs through his hard, blue eyes. "It's natural for dogs to be afraid of strangers."

Mr. Thomas nodded, though Mutt heard him say under his breath that this wasn't always true; the dogs hadn't reacted to any other human like this.

"What are their names?" Raymond asked in a quiet voice.

It hadn't been long since Mutt had heard the little girl Lisa ask the same question. But coming from Raymond, the words became ominous.

"That big guy is called Chief," said Mr. Thomas with fondness in his voice. "He's a strong fellow. And that little one, with the mark on her eye, she's Luna. You should see her dance."

Without comment, Raymond turned to the dogs and said, "C'mon, Chief and Luna, say hello to Raymond."

He had reached into his pocket and pulled out a handful of dog biscuits. None of the dogs had ever had treats like that before, and the smell was irresistible. The puppies and their mother ran over to Raymond, barking with excitement. Mutt couldn't help it, even as she told herself to keep her distance from this stranger.

Holding his hand out of reach, Raymond said, "Sit."

The dogs ignored him, staring up at the hand holding the treats.

His voice got even quieter.

"Sit," he whispered.

Mr. Thomas shook his head. "I don't think that's going to work with this group," he said.

Raymond turned to stare at him with a disdainful look that silenced the farmer.

Mutt felt uneasy, but she obeyed the stranger's command. The puppies did too. One by one they sat. One by one Raymond gave them a treat.

Mutt chewed and swallowed with reluctant pleasure. She couldn't resist this man's offerings, but she still didn't like him.

The puppies began barking for another treat.

This time, when Raymond said, "Sit," they immediately obeyed. Mutt tried to walk away but couldn't. The smell of the biscuits was too powerful. Growling, she returned to Raymond and sat next to her puppies, waiting for her turn.

But this time he didn't deliver the biscuits to their mouths. He tossed them into the cage on the wagon.

The puppies hesitated.

"Are we supposed to sit or go for them?" Luna asked her mother.

Before Mutt could answer, Raymond did. "Go on," he said. "Get 'em."

As the puppies scrambled into the cage, Mutt was overcome by fear and anger. She began to run after them, to pull them to safety. But before she reached them, Raymond slammed the door shut.

"Sorry, big Mama," he said in a flat tone. "I don't want you."

Mutt ran up to the cage and began to bark. Luna and Chief yelped back as they pressed their faces against the wire.

Without saying a word, Raymond grabbed the skin on the back of Mutt's neck and flipped her onto the ground.

"Stay," he commanded. Mutt lay there, panting in terror.

Mr. Thomas looked shocked. "Hey there, is that necessary?" he asked.

Raymond put his hand on the latch, securing the cage.

"She isn't hurt, just startled," he said. "Obviously no one has trained her." Then he added calmly, "I'm happy to leave the puppies here."

Mutt looked at Mr. Thomas, hoping he would summon the courage to reclaim the pups. But she realized immediately that Raymond was a bully who used fear as a weapon.

"Go on," Mr. Thomas said, shaking his head sadly.

"Take the puppies. You make sure they find a good home like you said, understand?"

"I understand," Raymond said in an even tone. "It's hard to say good-bye."

Mutt's instincts kicked in. She ran up to Raymond and began to bark furiously. But instead of leaping on him, the way she pounced on the fisher cat, she stood still, trapped by a feeling of helplessness. Later, she would ask herself over and over why she didn't attack him. But she had no answer. This man had some deep power she didn't comprehend.

She saw that Mr. Thomas shared her sense of helplessness. He turned his back while Raymond rolled the wagon toward his truck, parked out by the road.

As the truck disappeared from view, Mutt heard the sounds of Luna and Chief calling out to her, and then they grew fainter and fainter, until the air was still. She couldn't stop shaking as Mr. Thomas knelt beside her, stroking her neck.

The farmer pulled himself to his feet and began to walk back to the house. His shoulders were more stooped than usual.

"C'mon, Mutt," he said. "It's just you and me and Butch now."

chapter eleven

A TERRIBLE JOURNEY

L una howled in fury as Raymond loaded the cage holding her and Chief onto the back of the truck. Through her dread and anger she saw Raymond studying them without emotion, unimpressed by the noise they made.

She stared directly at him, her shyness overcome by her fierce desire to break free and run back to Mutt.

The man stared right back, and spoke with chilling authority. "Quiet," he said. "Quiet. You'll see your mother soon. We're just going for a ride." Then he climbed into the cab of the truck and turned on the engine.

Luna quieted from howls to whimpers, and as the truck began to move, she whispered to Chief, "Do you think he was telling the truth? About seeing our mother soon?"

Chief hesitated only a second, but to Luna it seemed like it took him forever to answer.

"Why would he bother to lie to us?" he replied. "He doesn't care about us."

Luna was willing to believe him. Chief's words were easier to accept than the alternative, that they would never see their mother again.

As the truck bumped along, Luna lay next to her brother on the hard floor of the cage. Through the wire mesh she could see the sky, changing colors as day melted into night. Despite the terrifying, jarring events of the day, and the uncertainty ahead, she curled up next to Chief and fell asleep. She was very tired.

It was dark when she and Chief were jolted awake. The truck had turned onto a rocky road.

"Whoa," called out Luna, after a big bump sent her flying to the top of the cage. The puppies were flopping all over each other, the way they did when they were wrestling. Only this wasn't fun.

They were too tired and scared to bark—until the truck stopped.

Disoriented, Luna and her brother opened their mouths and yapped loudly. Somehow Luna thought that Mutt might hear them.

A door slammed, and then came that now-familiar voice, barely audible, drowning her hopes like a dreary drizzle of rain.

"Quiet," Raymond grunted. "You'll get the whole place in an uproar."

He dragged the cage to the edge of the truck and yanked it onto the same wagon he had brought with him to Mr. Thomas's farm.

The puppies couldn't see that well in the dark, but they could smell. Luna's nose filled with a terrible stench.

This insult to her senses was quickly overwhelmed by something much worse.

"Ouch!" cried Luna as she felt a sting. "What's that?"

"Oh, no!" cried Chief. "Ouch!"

A swarm of fleas had descended. But Luna didn't know that this was what was happening to them. She didn't realize that back on their farm, Penny and her chicks had protected the dogs from attacks like this.

When the birds were clucking and chirping and running around, they were also eating little pests like the ones that were nipping at the puppies right now.

"Stop that noise," Raymond said, and he sprayed them with something from a can.

Then he walked away from them, and Luna heard a door open.

"Welcome to your new home," said Raymond, with a voice so cold that she and her brother both shivered. He wheeled them inside, into utter darkness.

chapter twelve

PUPPY PARADISE

L una felt a big thump as Raymond dropped them on the ground. He walked away without a word, leaving them on the other side of the door, trapped inside the cage.

Mutt had taught them early to keep the area where they slept nice and clean. That was impossible now. They couldn't hold their pee and poop forever.

"This is humiliating," whispered Luna, unable to hold it in any longer.

"More like disgusting," grumbled Chief.

Then he reassured his sister, as if he'd remembered he had to be strong.

"C'mon, Luna," he said, "let's make the best of this for now. We'll figure it out in the morning." He drew an imaginary line across the middle of the cage with his paw. His sister couldn't see it, but she stayed close enough to Chief to get what he was doing.

"Okay," he said. "We'll sleep on this side of the line. Everything else happens on the other side."

Before she could reply, a thin, snarly voice piped up in the dark.

"Okay, Luna," it said, making fun of Chief. "Get your good-night kiss over here; get ready for a big bowl of food over there. Take a refreshing dip in the lake over there too!"

A chorus of howls joined in.

"Oh yes, dear, welcome to Puppy Paradise, everything you could dream of!" someone shouted out.

The words may have been teasing, but the voices were grim.

Luna huddled against her brother.

"Chief, who's out there?" she whispered.

The unseen voices screamed back. "Chief! What is that?" they mocked.

"Welcome to your new home!" someone shouted.

Luna felt crushed by the waves of spite. Where had Raymond brought them? And why?

She and Chief crouched down as though they believed they could make themselves so small, their tormentors wouldn't know they were there. Even though it was so dark, no one could see anyway.

Then Luna thought of something that made her feel as though the darkness wouldn't swallow her.

She heard Mutt's voice inside her head.

"You will find your talent," Mutt had promised. "You are more like me than you know." Luna couldn't explain it, but she felt more positive, just remembering.

"Let's go to sleep," she said to her brother, not bothering to lower her voice. "We'll make some plans in the morning."

Her words set off another round of hoots from the unseen crowd.

"Good idea, dear!" one of the strangers yelled. "Get some sleep so you'll be rested for the exciting things you'll be doing tomorrow. Good idea!"

"Did you hear that?" asked Chief, as if the noise weren't deafening.

Luna was so exhausted she had already half drifted into sleep, on the clean side of the cage. She rearranged herself to allow Chief to curl up next to her, just as they did at home. His warm body was comforting. She fell asleep thinking about the farm.

That peaceful illusion lasted until morning. They were definitely not at home, but in a dank, dark barn, where light barely filtered in through the large cracks in the walls. Their cage was one of dozens, haphazardly placed on the ground; some perched precariously on hay bales.

Luna felt relief and pity when she saw who had been unnerving them so much the night before. The other cages were occupied by dogs, most of them small, all of them skinny and matted with filth. In the dim light of morning they lost their ferocity and lay limp and lifeless, as though the spirit had been drained out of them.

A gray mass of dirty fur lying in a nearby cage began to move.

A pair of eyes blinked and a voice emerged.

"Sorry about last night," it said. "The fellows who have been here a long time are so beaten down, they get their kicks by banging on the newcomers."

When Luna didn't respond, the gray fur added: "That's you."

The voice wasn't unfriendly, so Luna took a chance.

"What's your name?" she asked.

Gray Fur laughed in response, a bitter laugh.

"What's my name?" he repeated, as though Luna were speaking a foreign language. "What's my name? Good question. It's been so long since anyone called me by my name that I can barely remember. Here it's usually Scumdog, Filthymutt, Loser."

Chief stirred in his sleep.

Luna whispered, "But what's your actual name?"

She remembered how important she had felt when Gilbert called her Luna for the first time. Just a few months had passed, but it seemed very long ago.

Gray Fur slowly pulled himself to sit, stirring up a cloud of dust. Now that Luna's eyes had grown accustomed to the poor lighting, she could see that Gray Fur was a mess, barely recognizable as a dog.

"Charlie," he said. "My name was Charlie."

A voice interrupted him. "SHUT UP!" it shouted. "WE'RE TRYING TO SLEEP."

Charlie growled. "Shut up yourself," he snapped. "All anyone does here is sleep."

Chief muttered, "How lazy can you get?"

"Don't be too hard on them," Charlie said. "Some of us have been here for months, waiting to get out. Then newbies like you come in and hurt our chances. It's hard not to become bitter."

Neither Chief nor Luna knew how to respond. Luna felt sympathy for Charlie and the other dogs. But she didn't want to stay in this place one second longer than she had to.

Her nostrils flared. "How do you stand the stench?" she asked.

Charlie seemed perplexed. "What stench?"

"What *stench*?" Chief shuddered. "Aren't you breathing?"

"That's about all I do," said Charlie. "You learn not to smell or think, or you'll go crazy."

Luna asked, "But why are we here? Why are *you* here?"

Charlie pressed his face against the wires of his cage.

"We're here because we're adorable puppies for sale," he said in a mocking tone. "Here at Puppy Paradise."

Luna looked around. She saw cages full of sad-sack dogs. Some had tangled fur like Charlie's. They were in the best shape. Others had ugly patches of red skin and runny eyes. All of them were bony, with hollowed-out chests and concave stomachs.

Who would want them? she thought to herself.

Charlie read her mind. "You're probably thinking, *Who would want them?*" he said. "Good question. That's why we're still here—for now."

Luna was confused.

Charlie explained. "Raymond specializes in selling puppies that aren't purebreds but are well behaved," he said. "We're the ones that won't bow down to him."

Chief's head drooped. He seemed even wearier all of a sudden. "What does he want?" he growled.

Charlie replied, "Total obedience."

"What happens if you're well behaved?" Luna asked.

Charlie corrected her. "If *Raymond* thinks you're well behaved."

Luna blinked.

Charlie answered her question. "You get to go to the other barn, the one people see on the brochure. You get cleaned up and are expected to start mating, to produce puppies for Raymond to sell. By the time he takes you over there, you're broken. You'll do anything Raymond wants."

Chief's eyes widened. "What happens if you don't become totally obedient?" he asked.

Charlie hesitated.

"Sometimes dogs just disappear," he said. "Maybe they get to go home. But there have been rumors . . ."

"Rumors of what?" Chief had shaken off his drowsiness and was alert.

Charlie lowered his head. "I hate to say," he replied.

"Say it," commanded Chief, who was so accustomed to being the big brother that he acted as if everyone would obey him.

Charlie lowered his voice. "I don't know all the awful truth of this place," he said. "But I've heard that sometimes dogs just get dumped by the side of the road."

His voice became ominous. "Or worse."

Just then the barn door opened. All the dogs, including Charlie, fell silent.

chapter thirteen

HARSH LESSONS

Raymond walked in, accompanied by a hand-some Rottweiler, a powerful-looking dog with an arrogant look on his face.

"That dog looks like Raymond's twin," Luna whispered.

"Don't insult the dog," Chief whispered back.

Luna looked gratefully at Chief. "I'm glad you haven't lost your sense of humor," she said.

"Shhh," warned Charlie.

Luna and Chief watched in silence as dog and man began to walk by the cages, opening each one as they passed it. None of the imprisoned dogs moved a muscle, even though they had been cramped inside for hours.

Luna sniffed the air. The smell of food had pierced the stink that blanketed the barn. She noticed that Raymond was carrying a large bag.

We're going to be fed, she thought with relief.

She resisted the urge to bark eagerly, the way she and her siblings used to greet Gilbert and then Mr. Thomas when they brought them dinner. It took all of her willpower not to press herself against the cage, trying to get closer to the reassuring smell.

She saw Chief look at her, a warning in his eye. Luna lowered her head, to let him know she understood that there was a rule to be obeyed, even though she didn't quite know what the rule was or why it existed.

The silence was broken by an outburst of barking, accompanied by a jarring human laugh.

Cautiously Luna peered toward the noise.

One of those poor, pathetic creatures—she could barely think of them as dogs—couldn't help himself. His hunger had overcome his willpower and his fear. He had jumped out of the cage and run over to the bag of food Raymond was carrying.

"Teach him a lesson, Hades," Raymond said to the Rottweiler, who instantly obeyed. He bit down on the neck of the poor animal and started shaking him like a rag doll.

All the other dogs watched, misery in their eyes. None moved to interfere, not even the ones whose cage doors had been opened.

Luna could feel the tension ripple through the barn as she and the other trapped dogs fought their primal instinct, forcing themselves to sit motionless. Her sense of helplessness stung like a slap, more painful than the hunger that was gripping her insides, or the anxiety that was squeezing her breath.

Chief placed his paw on hers and she placed one of hers on his. It was as though they were creating a chain of love to keep them strong.

"You two catch on quickly," Charlie whispered with quiet admiration.

Finally, Raymond reached over and touched Hades on the back.

"Let him be," Raymond said. "I think he learned his lesson."

Hades immediately opened his mouth and let the other dog drop to the ground, where he lay on his side, gasping for breath.

Raymond pulled on a pair of work gloves and leaned over to pick up the panting dog, who was covered with scratches from Hades' teeth. The cuts were minor, but Luna knew that the deepest wounds aren't always physical.

"That'll teach you," Raymond snapped as he tossed the dog back in his cage, slammed the door shut, and latched it. "No food for you today."

Luna watched him squat next to the cage so that his eyes were level with the dog.

The dog lowered his eyes.

"Look at me," Raymond said softly.

The dog turned his eyes toward the man's.

"I'm doing this for your own good," Raymond said. "I will teach you to appreciate kindness, make you desperate for love and attention. That's what people want."

That's not true, Luna thought to herself. Gilbert was a person and he didn't use kindness as a reward. He was just kind. She wanted to please him because he encouraged her, not because he made her feel afraid.

Glancing at Chief, she could tell that he was thinking the same thing. He caught her eye and shook his head, just enough to warn her to remain still, to pretend she hadn't noticed the frightening cruelty taking place just a few steps away.

When Raymond reached their cage, he opened the door and waited.

The puppies didn't move.

"How did you enjoy your first night in your new home?" he asked.

Luna and Chief sat very still.

"Let me introduce you to your boss," Raymond continued. "This is Hades, king of his domain."

Hades glared at the puppies and growled, just to prove how tough he was.

They didn't need convincing. Neither of them moved a whisker.

Raymond's eyes revealed a flicker of respect.

"You catch on fast, don't you?" he said. "Maybe someone will actually want one of you mutts."

Luna's heart skipped when she heard her mother's name.

Then, through the fog of hunger and fright, she was pierced by the realization that there were a few pieces of dog food next to her paw.

She remembered what Charlie had said the night before: Total obedience was the way out of here.

Luna didn't know how she restrained herself. But she did. Once again she thought of Gilbert, and the patient way he had taught her to do tricks.

"You have to concentrate," he would tell her.

So she willed herself to look like a statue from the outside, while inside she was squirming with desire for the food that was right there.

For a few minutes that felt like forever, she didn't move, not even her eyes, ignoring Raymond and Hades, who stood on the other side of the barn watching her and her brother, waiting for them to give in to their hunger.

Luna ignored the dust that made her feel like sneezing, and resisted the urge to look at Chief, to see if he was also holding himself back. She silently sang the words to Gilbert's song about the moon eating olives and pretended she was lying in the grass, exhausted from running through the fields.

Then she felt, rather than heard, Raymond's words.
"C'mon, Hades, let's get out of here," he said.

As Hades passed their cage he growled. "We'll see how long your willpower lasts," he taunted them.

The puppies ignored him.

They didn't budge until Raymond and Hades left the barn and shut the door behind them. Then they gobbled up their pathetic dinner.

"How will we survive on this little bit of food?" Luna asked Chief mournfully. "I'm soooo hungry."

"We're all hungry," Chief said.

Luna lowered her head in shame.

Chief nuzzled her.

"We have to stay strong," he said. "Like Mother. Remember what she told us: 'You are more like me than you know.'"

Luna forgot her hunger for a minute.

"She said that to *you* too?" Luna felt her spirits fall even lower.

Chief laughed. "I heard her say it to Alegre and Happy too."

Luna didn't want to ask the next question, but she couldn't help herself. "Did she promise you anything?"

"The same thing she promised you," he said. "That I would find my talent."

Luna couldn't believe her ears.

"How could she do that?" she asked. "How could she promise us the same thing?"

Chief laid his head on his sister's. "Why do you think, Luna?" he asked gently.

Luna thought for a minute. "Because that's what she hoped?" she asked.

Before Chief could answer, the barn door opened again.

chapter fourteen

LOUIS

O h, no," whispered Luna. "Now what?"

It was hard to make out who was walking through the barn. The light was dim, even in daytime, and Luna found that her usually acute sense of smell was blocked by the strong odor inside.

Her ears perked up. Cage by cage, dogs began rustling around, unafraid to make noise. Some of them even gave weak barks of greeting.

Luna felt brave enough to ask Charlie, "Who is that?"

"That's Raymond's helper," said Charlie. "His name is Louis. He's just a kid and not so bad. He's never mean unless Raymond is around. He does all the dirty work. Every few days we get to go outside into a pen while Louis cleans out the barn. And his other job . . ."

Charlie fell silent.

"What?" barked Luna.

Charlie muttered, "You'll find out soon enough."

Louis walked over to Luna and Chief's cage. He had soft brown eyes that reminded Luna of Gilbert.

"Sorry, puppies," he said.

He disappeared for a minute and returned carrying a machine of some kind. He opened their cage door and then pulled Luna out with both hands and wrapped her in a big towel, so only her head stuck out.

Louis checked something on a piece of paper he pulled from his pocket. Then he looked at the puppy's face.

"You are Luna, I can see that," he said, touching the moon-shaped mark above her eye.

She whimpered.

Louis said gently, "Raymond told me your names."

Then he took a belt and wrapped it around Luna so her legs were trapped tight inside the towel. He pulled out a razor and, before Luna knew what was

happening, he shaved the fur on the inside of her ear.
With shock more than pain, she yelped.

"Shhhh," said Louis. "You don't want Raymond to
hear. We'll both get into trouble."

He gently wiped her ear with alcohol and then
rubbed some Vaseline on the fresh pink skin.

Luna's eyes widened in terror.

"Don't be afraid, little one," said Louis.

The kindness in his voice calmed her down.

The next step in this procedure happened fast. Louis brought the machine to her head. There was a needle at the end of it, and he placed that needle against Luna's ear with one hand, while holding her steady with the other.

"L-U-N-A," he said as he printed her name on the inside of her ear with the sharp tool.

The needle pinched rather than hurt. Even if it had, Luna was too weak to object.

"This was my idea," Louis said as he stroked Luna's head. "I convinced Raymond to tattoo the puppies' *names* inside their ears, instead of numbers."

Luna whimpered again.

"No matter what happens, you'll have your name," Louis told her.

He jerked his head toward the door. "That makes me feel better about working for him."

Just then Raymond yelled from outside.

"What's taking you so long in there, boy?" he called out. "I've got other things for you to do."

"I'm almost done," Louis replied with humor in his voice. "These mutts have tough skin."

He winked at Luna as he put her back in the cage and took out Chief, who stepped into the towel and stood waiting.

"You're a smart one, aren't you?" said Louis. "Okay Chief, here we go."

Despite the stinging in Luna's ears, being around Louis made her feel hopeful.

Then Raymond called again, louder.

"Get out here now!" he yelled. "We have lots of work to do."

Louis locked the puppies back in their cage and began to walk away. Then he turned around.

"I know you must think I'm terrible for working here," he said. "But it's the only job I could get. I only wish . . ."

Before he could finish, Raymond called his name again.

"I have to go," Louis said, a shadow crossing his face. He left his wish unspoken, to Luna's disappointment.

Louis's sweet nature had cleared the air. It actually seemed to smell better in the barn. But the instant he left, gloom descended.

"Nothing has changed," Luna whispered to Chief. "Louis is nice, but he can't make this loathsome place any better."

111

Chief swatted Luna with his paw.

"C'mon, Luna," he said. "Show Charlie how you can dance."

Luna sank to the bottom of the cage and shook her head.

But Chief didn't give up. He kept poking her until she got to her feet, just to make him stop.

Somehow she found room in that tiny space to move her feet the way Gilbert had taught her. Somehow, she was able to remember the moon and hoped it still existed, somewhere out there.

chapter fifteen

WHAT LUNA REALIZED

It didn't take long for them to lose track of time. Luna could barely remember what it had been like to go out and play whenever they felt like it. Their new "home" was a prison.

Once every few days the dogs were taken outside to a closed-in pen while Louis came in to clean out the barn. Most of the dogs were too weak to do anything but lie down in the sun, shivering in the brisk winter air. Chief forced Luna to run around.

"We have to be ready," he told her.

"For what?" she asked him.

"For whatever might happen," he said.

Charlie became a friend—the only friend they found in this miserable place. They were shocked to discover he was only a few months older than they were. He sagged like an old dog, even though he was not much more than a pup.

He told them stories about where he'd come from. Like them, he'd had a good life until one day the people who owned him had to move. They took his mother with them but gave away her puppies, including Charlie. Charlie missed his mother but liked his new owners—for the short time he was with them. Something happened that changed their plans and then Raymond showed up at the door.

Charlie taught them the ropes. He told them which dogs to avoid and how to keep Hades from bothering them.

"Let him know you respect him but don't look him in the eye," Charlie said one day, during a rare moment in the sun. "Don't let him know you're scared of him but don't make him think you aren't."

Chief hadn't lost his sense of humor. He poked Charlie with his nose, and asked, "How do we manage that? It's like saying, 'Smack him in the face, but don't hit him.' 'Despise him, but show him you like him.' 'Be quiet, but bark.'"

At first Charlie looked hurt, but then he realized Chief was teasing.

"You remind me of my brother," he said to Chief. "He was a tease too."

Then he lowered his voice. "You have the right idea," he whispered. "I know it's another of my contradictions, but it's good to keep your sense of humor without forgetting this is a dangerous place."

Things brightened momentarily whenever Louis showed up to clean the barn. He reminded the dogs that there were humans who weren't hateful. He was brave too, sneaking them treats even though he knew he would probably be fired if Raymond found out.

Most important, Louis gave them hope.

"Remember Miranda?" he'd say to the dogs when he opened their cages. "The black terrier that was here for a while? Some nice people came to get her."

He never mentioned the dogs whose stories didn't have happy endings.

Louis never said anything bad about his boss, but the dogs could tell that he didn't like the way they were treated.

"It's disgusting in here," he would say when he came to clean the barn. "Don't worry, I'll make it as nice as I can."

Luna could tell that Louis did his best to rake out the filth. For a day or two the barn would be bearable.

Even Hades acted different when he came to the barn with Louis. The guard dog still growled and looked tough, but he didn't bite or bully any of the dogs. Sometimes he almost looked sad, like he realized he was a traitor to his own kind.

The worst times were when Raymond walked through the door. Luckily, he rarely came into the barn. When he did, it meant someone was coming or going. These were always terrible moments. Luna and her brother became accustomed to watching newcomers endure their first exposure to this unhappy place without offering a word of comfort. They felt themselves change. They had been good-natured puppies accustomed to love, but now they knew they had to harden their hearts or they would be destroyed.

It was almost as bad watching a puppy being taken out. Maybe the puppy had escaped to a better life, like the ones Louis told them about. But what if it hadn't?

At first Chief talked a lot about what would happen when they got out. But day by day it became harder to dream. It takes strength to dream, and the puppies were growing weaker.

Then quite by accident, Louis gave them back their strength.

He was working in the barn when he began to sing quietly to himself.

When Luna heard Louis sing, she felt her feet begin to move. She had stopped thinking about their cozy haven under Gilbert's house, but now her feet were remembering for her! Only a few months had passed since those lovely days, but it seemed like forever. It hurt to think about what she had left behind, but it also reminded her of who she was.

"Chief," she said to her brother with remarkable assertiveness, considering her weakened condition. "We have to get out of here."

chapter sixteen

BACK ON THE FARM

Mutt carried on the way she always had. She patrolled the farm, as she promised Mr. Thomas she would.

When she finished her rounds, she often stopped to visit Penny.

"How's your empty nest?" Penny would ask Mutt with a cackle.

Sometimes Mutt confessed she worried about her offspring. Penny reassured her. "They will take care of themselves," she said. "You gave them part of you, and that's a great deal."

The chicken always asked, "How's that cat treating you?" Penny wasn't a fan of Butch.

"He isn't exactly dog's best friend, but he's okay," said Mutt. "When it got cold, Mr. Thomas invited me to stay inside the house. Butch has his places and I have mine. It feels like peace to me."

The dog noticed the way the winter sun bounced off Penny's copper-colored feathers.

"Your feathers look very pretty in this light," Mutt said.

Penny lowered her head modestly.

"Thank you," she said. "And how is Mr. Thomas?"

Mutt thought for a minute.

"He said the most remarkable thing the other night," she said, "just sitting in his chair talking to the cat."

Penny ran around in circles and chortled, "Talking to the cat?"

Mutt nodded.

"What did he say?" the chicken asked.

"He said, 'I should have waited for another little girl or boy like Lisa to come along to take care of the puppies the right way.'"

Mutt paused and cleared her throat.

Penny squatted on the ground, waiting for Mutt to continue.

"He looked at me and said, 'I know I did the wrong thing. I just got impatient and when Raymond came around looking for puppies I trusted him even though I didn't believe he was trustworthy.'"

Mutt sighed. "I must have groaned a little, because Mr. Thomas said he was sure Raymond would find a good home for poor little Luna and Chief—but I could tell he didn't believe his own words."

Penny began to cluck sympathetically.

"It must be hard for you, not knowing where your puppies have gone," she said.

"I tried to make them strong enough to face the world," Mutt said, feeling sad. "But the world keeps changing. I don't know if they're prepared."

"How can you ever know?" Penny asked.

The two friends sat in a companionable silence for a couple of minutes, thinking about the mysteries of existence.

Then Penny shook her feathers.

"I have to go," she said.

Penny turned to leave and then stopped to say one more thing.

"Don't worry about your puppies," she said. "You've taught them more than you know."

Mutt felt more cheerful than she had in some time

as she walked to the mailbox, which she nudged open with her nose. (Picking up the mail had become one of her chores after the puppies left.) She grabbed the few pieces of paper with her teeth and carried them up to the house.

Mr. Thomas was waiting for her by the front door.

"Good dog," he said, taking the letters from her mouth. He held the door open and Mutt walked inside.

She lay at Mr. Thomas's feet while he opened the mail. Just as she was about to fall asleep, the farmer startled her by tossing a piece of crumpled paper on the floor, right next to her tail. He seemed upset. Mutt sat up and placed her paw on his knee, hoping to make him feel better.

Mr. Thomas scratched her ears and sighed. Then he leaned over and picked up the paper.

"Listen to this, Mutt," he said.

Mutt paid close attention as Mr. Thomas began to read.

> Dear Mr. Thomas,
>
> I hope you are fine. Please read this letter to Mutt and the puppies. Tell them I miss them very much and am sad we won't see them next summer. Tell them I love them. Tell Luna by herself I would like her to come to New York. It is scary but there is a lot to see. Make sure the others don't hear but tell her I miss her the most and think of her every time I see the moon in the sky. And tell Mutt thank you for changing my life.
>
> Thank you.
> Gilbert

Mutt's heart raced when she heard Mr. Thomas mention Luna and Gilbert. Without realizing it, her tail had begun to thump against the floor.

Mr. Thomas leaned down to stroke her fur. With an emotional voice he said, "Like Gilbert wrote, thank you for changing my life."

chapter seventeen

THE GREAT ESCAPE

L una surprised herself with her declaration of independence. Until that moment she hadn't realized how hungry she was, though she had become uncomfortably aware that her ribs had begun to press against her skin. She often fell asleep wondering how long she would be able to endure Puppy Paradise.

Yet just saying the words "We have to get out of here" sent a jolt of energy through her body, as though she'd had an actual meal instead of pathetic scraps. Just thinking of escape made her remember she was Mutt's puppy, daughter of a hero, not a bully's punching bag.

As these thoughts ran through her head, Chief licked her face.

"You are right!" he said, his voice filled with excitement and brotherly pride.

Then he spit.

"And you are filthy!" he added, the old teasing Chief back in his voice.

The siblings began to plot and scheme, keeping their voices as low as possible so no one would hear.

Charlie sensed that something was up.

"What are you two always whispering about?" he asked on one of those rare days when they were outside, while Louis cleaned the barn.

Luna looked at the ground and at Chief, a question mark in her eyes.

"Can't we tell him?" Chief asked Luna. His attitude toward her had changed since she had the nerve to say out loud the words he had only dared to dream. He looked to Luna to lead the way.

She paced back and forth, thinking. She stopped to stare at Charlie. Standing in the sunlight, with no shadows to hide the straw and sticks and dirt tangled in his fur, their friend managed to look even scragglier than usual.

"All right," Luna sighed, putting her face close to Charlie's. "But this is strictly between us."

As she muttered their plan to Charlie, Louis came outside with Hades. The unfriendly guard dog planted himself right in front of Luna and Charlie.

"What are you two mutts plotting," he growled.

Charlie shook the fur out of his eyes and began to speak.

Luna listened to him in disbelief.

"We're planning the great escape," Charlie said sarcastically, looking Hades right in the eye.

He lifted his paw and poked Hades in the chest.

"Wanna come with us?"

As Luna held her breath, Hades swatted away Charlie's paw and barked in disgust.

"You have always been ridiculous," he said to Charlie.

He added, "Now, what were you really talking about? Tell me or I'll—"

Charlie lowered his head in mock fear. "I'm sorry, Hades," he said. "I didn't mean to show any disrespect. I was just making a joke."

Hades ignored the apology.

"Just answer me," he barked.

Charlie said, "Do I have to?"

Hades glared.

"Okay," said Charlie submissively. "I was just telling Luna here that I felt sure I was going to be adopted soon. Just a feeling I had."

Hades rolled over on his back, barking with laughter. All the dogs in the pen stared in wonder. They had never seen the formidable dog show any emotion besides anger.

"That's the funniest thing I ever heard," said Hades, unable to stop laughing as he said these cruel words. "Who would want *you?*"

He jumped to his feet and bared his teeth at Charlie, who couldn't stop himself from quaking.

As Hades erupted in laughter again, Chief began shaking with rage.

Luna gave her brother a warning look as Hades walked over and shoved his large face right up against Charlie's.

"Oh, yeah, brave warrior," he said. "Someone is going to want to adopt an ugly, miserable, weak sack of fur like you."

He backed away, laughing again.

Louis came out of the barn. "I'm done in there," he said, wiping his forehead. "Whew."

He wandered over and patted Hades on the head.

"I never saw Hades pay attention to any of you dogs when he wasn't punishing you," he said with a smile. "Good dog, Hades."

Louis turned to Charlie and patted him too.

"Good work, Charlie," he said. "I see you've made Hades your friend. That's something!"

Hades stepped closer to Charlie and opened his mouth, in a way that resembled a human smile. "How easy humans are to fool," Hades growled. "Good work, Charlie."

Charlie stood there quivering as Hades followed Louis back into the barn.

"Take it easy, Charlie," Luna said. "He's not worth it."

Charlie winked at her.

"I know that," he said with a grin. "He fell right into my trap."

Luna saw Chief's jaw drop.

"Good work, Charlie," she said, but unlike Hades, she meant it.

Louis whistled. This was the signal for the dogs to go back inside, back into their cages.

Luna could tell that whatever doubts Charlie may have had about escaping had been blown away by his encounter with Hades. Weeks of imprisonment had taken their toll on the once-feisty dog, but it was obvious that his spirit had been reignited.

Day by day, the three friends added details to their escape plan. They had plenty of time until Louis came to clean out the barn again. They exercised in their cages at night, lying on their backs and waving their legs in the air, in order to build up their strength. Luna taught them dance steps, to keep them moving when they thought they couldn't.

They exercised their minds too, with tricks and games. One of them would give a short bark, mimicking Hades, and the others would mentally take off, trying to see how little time could elapse between hearing the bark and their legs starting to move.

When Louis finally came back to clean out the barn, they were ready.

Charlie called Hades over to him in the outside pen.

"Hades," he said coyly. "I felt we were really starting to bond last time you were here."

Hades looked at him with puzzlement in his eyes.

"What are you talking about?" he barked.

As he walked over to Charlie, his throat rumbling with a threatening growl, Luna and Chief edged toward the entry to the barn, lightly moving one paw after the other.

"Really, Hades, I feel I can tell you my innermost thoughts," said Charlie. "I think we can become friends."

The gamble paid off, just as they had predicted it would. Hades began roaring with laughter, his sides shaking so hard, he rolled onto his back, just as he had done before.

The instant Hades hit the ground, Charlie took off running. Luna and Chief were already racing through the barn toward the open door on the other side.

"Can you believe we're doing it?!" Charlie yelled giddily.

This was no practice, no game in a cage. Now they were running for real, with only a second's notice.

Before Hades or Louis realized what was happening, the weary prisoners had turned into speed racers. They zoomed through the barn and out the front door, which Louis always left open to air out the barn while he cleaned it. When they were all on the other side, Chief pushed the outside door closed with his butt. Luna scrambled onto his back and nudged down the latch with her nose.

Louis and Hades were locked inside, just as the puppies had planned.

Hades' angry barking was growing fainter. As they ran, Luna noticed a neat red barn out of the corner of her eye. It must be the one Charlie had told them about, where people come to choose their puppies.

"Look at that!" she barked in surprise.

Chief huffed, "There's no time. Run!"

Charlie was wheezing. Before they reached the main road, he had begun to fall behind.

Luna glanced backward and yelled out to him. "C'mon, Charlie! You can do this."

He picked up his pace. Soon they felt hard pavement beneath their feet.

"We did it!" Chief yelled.

"Not yet," Luna said grimly, panting hard. "Don't even think of slowing down. We have to put as much distance between us and them as we can."

She heard Charlie start to moan. She knew his legs were shorter than hers and Chief's, and he had been in Puppy Paradise so much longer than they had.

But she soon realized that Charlie was determined not to go back.

"C'mon, everyone," he barked.

The sun was bright overhead. Luna felt her senses

133

come alive again. Occasionally as they ran, one of the dogs would bark, not saying anything at all, just exercising the right to speak without being shushed or yelled at.

Luna felt as though she could run forever, as though gravity no longer held her down. Nothing distracted her or the other two dogs. Not the farmland stretching back from the road. Not the fields still brown from winter. Not the birds racing above them, cheering them on with their tweets and twitters. Not the familiar sounds of cows mooing. They were beyond thought. They had become machines, programmed to get as far away from Puppy Paradise as they possibly could. Nothing else mattered.

Luna was the first to feel the road vibrating beneath her paws.

"What's that?" she asked, trying not to panic.

Chief glanced back.

"Run faster!" he barked, terror in his voice.

But to Luna and Chief's shock, Charlie stopped in his tracks.

"I'm too tired," he said, his voice so quiet they could barely hear him. "It's over for me, friends. You go ahead."

A minute later Raymond's truck pulled up next to Charlie. Hades was sitting in the passenger seat, a smug grin on his face. As Luna glanced back, she saw Charlie look at the ground. She knew he must be thinking of how to drag out his capture long enough for her and her brother to get away.

But Raymond didn't waste any time. He didn't even bother to let Hades out of the truck. The man jumped out and, without wasting a motion, dropped a feed sack over Charlie's whole body. He tossed him into the back of the truck, jumped into the driver's seat, and roared onward.

Luna was in shock. Exhilaration had turned to despair in an instant. As she heard the truck bump up and down the road behind her, she began to bark, "Go faster, Chief."

The truck came closer. She heard Charlie barking, "Please don't catch them, please don't catch them."

Then she heard another, horrible voice: Hades. "Shut up back there. You're a bunch of losers."

Luna heard the screech of the truck's brakes. "Keep running!" she yelled to Chief.

But the next thing she knew she was struggling inside darkness. Raymond had caught her just as he'd caught Charlie.

"Luna?"

Her heart sank when she heard Chief's voice. None of them had escaped.

Then Raymond spoke.

"You are a bunch of ingrates," he said in a grim voice. "I'm the only one who can help you, and this is how you pay me back? I thought you were about ready to move on. But I see you'll need extra training when we get back."

The puppies tried to claw their way out, but Raymond had tied the sacks shut too tight. Not even Hades would be able to shake it loose, much less puppies who had used all their strength trying to escape.

They heard Raymond slam the truck's tailgate, get into the front, and begin to drive. Then they heard something else: a banging sound that they would soon discover was the tailgate, bouncing up and down as the truck roared toward Puppy Paradise. Raymond had forgotten to close the latch!

chapter eighteen
ON THE ROAD

The frightened puppies jostled against one another in the dark as the truck swerved from side to side. Suddenly there was an enormous jolt, as if the road had opened up and tried to swallow them. The sacks holding the puppies went flying across the tailgate and rolled onto the side of the road.

Shocked and numb with pain, Luna listened to the truck roar off in the distance.

When the noise died down, Luna called out.

"Chief? Charlie? Are you here? Are you all right?"

A muffled bark, Charlie's, replied. "I think I'm right next to you."

"Me too," groaned Chief.

As though someone had blown the starting whistle, all the puppies began to scratch at the bags confining them.

Luna felt something bang into her ribs.

"Ouch!" she yelled. "What is that?"

"That's me!" Chief replied.

"Stop poking me," Luna snapped.

"It was an accident," Chief muttered.

They were interrupted by the sound of laughter—weak, but laughter all the same.

It was Charlie.

"If the last thing I hear on earth is the two of you squabbling, it will almost be worth it," he said.

"What are you talking about, Charlie?" asked Luna, still dazed from being thrown out of the truck and uncertain as to what was going on.

"Don't you see," said Charlie's voice in the dark. "We're free to say whatever we want!"

"Be quiet, Charlie," said Luna with a mixture of affection and annoyance. "We may be free to say what we want, but if we don't get out of these sacks before Raymond figures out he doesn't have us, we'll be finished."

They squirmed and wriggled, scratched and bit. But the heavy canvas was stronger than they were.

"Why haven't they come back?" Chief wondered out loud.

"It's dark and they probably figure we'll be here in the morning," Charlie said. "Or maybe . . ."

"Maybe what?" asked Luna.

Charlie muttered, "Maybe they figured we're not worth the trouble."

Luna was about to answer when her canvas prison started to rustle. "What's that?" she whispered, just as Charlie called out, "Hey, are you guys moving around over there?"

Luna was too scared to answer.

Charlie called out again. This time he sounded desperate.

"Is that you?" he yelled.

Luna was confused. "I thought it was you!" she replied.

A burst of high-pitched chatter set off a shiver of fear down Luna's back. She heard a ripping sound and felt fresh air filter into the sack. At first she welcomed the breeze, but then the end of the sack started to jerk back and forth.

Feeling the presence of someone or something,

139

she jumped as far into the air as her tired legs and cramped space would allow.

"What's there?!" she yelled in alarm.

A tiny head—that appeared to be balanced on a large set of teeth—poked its way inside.

"Who are you?" asked the creature and Luna at the same time.

Another round of chatter was set off from another direction. Luna heard Charlie begin to bark like crazy. She and Chief joined in. Despite their fatigue, their voices were loud and strong.

"Are you fisher cats?" Luna screamed. Mutt's battle with the fisher cat was a family legend.

"Whoa, whoa, whoa!" called out the intruder who had chewed his way through Luna's sack. "Take it easy, pup. You have the wrong idea. I don't know what a fisher cat is, but we're not one of them."

Luna stopped barking and squinted at the creature. He was tiny, with black rings around his eyes and a light brown stripe down his back. His ears were nubs, almost nonexistent, but his cheeks were enormous.

Luna couldn't help it. She found herself grinning at this comical being, framed by moonlight.

"How did you get in here?" she asked. "I couldn't

make a dent in this . . ." She glanced around. "This . . . whatever it is."

"It's a feedbag," he said. Then he added, with pride in his voice, "See these teeth?"

Luna muttered, "Hard to miss!"

The newcomer ignored her. "These bright whites can chew through almost anything: wood, wires, cans."

He paused for effect.

"Canvas, that's nothing!" he scoffed.

Chief had wriggled out of his sack and was sitting next to Luna by then.

The weird little creature looked suspiciously at the puppies. "What are you fellows doing in here?" he asked. "I was hoping to find some food."

Chief growled. "Before we tell you, let's get out of here," he said. "Raymond may be coming back."

As the stranger asked, "Who's Raymond?" Luna and Chief made their way over to find Charlie, who was sitting on his sack next to another of these funny little creatures.

"Hey there," Charlie said. "This is Jack. He's a chipmunk."

"Chipmunk?" asked Luna.

"I've heard of chipmunks," Chief said. "You're rodents!"

Jack raised his miniature paws and curled them into fists. "You have a problem with that?" he asked.

Chief leaned toward Luna and muttered in her ear, "I've heard they're awful pests that eat just about anything."

Jack glanced from side to side, as though he was processing many rapid thoughts.

"You know what they say," he squealed. "One dog's pest is another dog's hero."

He lay on his back laughing.

"You'll have to excuse him," said the other chipmunk. "He loves his own jokes."

Then he began glancing from side to side, just like Jack. "Sorry to be rude," he said. "My name is Jackson."

"Are you kidding me?" Luna said with a giggle. "Jack and Jackson?"

Jackson shrugged. "It's the chipmunk way," he said mysteriously. "Sometimes we just call ourselves a pair of Jacks."

Chief took charge.

"Thanks a lot, you two," he said. "But we have to get on our way."

Luna looked wearily at her brother. Now that they had stopped, she realized how tired and hungry she was.

"Chief, I can't take another step without something to eat," she said. "I just can't."

Charlie nodded. "That goes double for me, champ," he said. "I don't have much fight left in me."

Jack scampered over to Jackson. They conferred in the same high-pitched chatter that had frightened Luna at first.

Then the chipmunks scooted back to the puppies.

"Here's the plan," Jackson said.

"I wasn't sure if we should do it," Jack confessed. "Spring isn't really here yet."

"And we are still scrounging for food," filled in Jackson.

"That's why we chomped through these bags," added Jack, nodding toward the crumpled sacks.

"You must have been scared in there," Jackson said.

"You think?" Jack replied. "Those sacks don't look so scary—"

"But it was dark," said Jackson.

Chief barked at them impatiently.

"Can you two get to the point?" he demanded.

"Whoa, whoa, whoa," Jackson and Jack said, more

or less together. "Who was it who rescued you?"

Luna interjected gently. "He—we—we're just hungry," she said. "We appreciate what you've done for us."

Chief tossed Luna a look filled with pride for her.

"You're right," he said, hanging his head.

"Sorry, sorry," Jackson said, glancing from side to side and back. "Just follow us."

They zoomed off, causing Charlie to shout, "Slow down."

"Right," said Jack. "Jackson, slow down!"

Within a few minutes they paused near a tree and began to dig. Soon they had unearthed a good-sized pile of nuts, seeds, crackers, and dried apples.

The dogs stared at this bounty in amazement.

"Don't just stare," Jack said. "Eat! It's on us."

The famished puppies began to devour the feast the chipmunks had spread out on the ground.

Chief gobbled an apple and then stopped.

"Don't eat too many nuts," he warned Luna and Charlie.

"Why not?" Luna asked. "They're delicious."

Chief replied, "I can't remember exactly, but someone—Mr. Thomas or Gilbert—said it wasn't good for dogs."

"Know-it-all," Luna grumbled. But she stopped eating the nuts and focused on the rest.

Their meal was interrupted by Jack and Jackson, who began to scamper again.

"Come on," they shouted. "Leave some for the rest of the winter."

This time the puppies didn't hesitate. For the next hour or two, they followed the chipmunks from one hidden treasure to another.

Along the way, Chief asked, "How did you know about all this?"

Jack replied, "We put them there!"

Jackson added, "That's what we do."

Stuffing his cheeks until they were about to pop, he explained. "See, we find some seeds and collect them in our cheeks," said Jackson.

"Our saliva is a kind of preservative," explained Jack. "That way we have food in storage all winter and it doesn't spoil."

"You were lucky," said Jackson. "We sleep most of the time when it's cold, but every once in a while we refill our bellies so we can continue to rest till spring. You just happened to catch us when we were out and about."

As Jackson was talking, Luna spit something out.

"What's that?" she said. "I can't bite through that seed."

Jack inspected the thing she spit out.

"Whoops, I'm sorry," he said. "That's an olive pit. You can't eat that."

Luna was struck by a strange feeling she couldn't describe. She didn't realize that the word "olive" reminded her of the song Gilbert used to sing to her.

The pleasant moment was interrupted by the sound of screeching tires in the distance.

"Raymond!" Luna exclaimed in terror.

"Follow us," said Jack and Jackson at the same time.

The puppies scrambled through the underbrush after the chipmunks, their way lit by moonlight, until the chipmunks suddenly disappeared.

"Where are they?" Charlie asked in a panic.

Jackson's—or Jack's—head popped up out of a hole.

"Come here!" he whispered. The puppies dived after him, into a huge tunnel that led underground.

When they finally stopped, the animals huddled together, trying to catch their breath.

Jack and Jackson stood up and bowed.

"Welcome to our burrow," Jack said. "You'll be safe here."

Before the puppies could properly say thank you, they had collapsed into the sweet slumber of freedom. For the first time in weeks, hope, not fear, ushered in sleep. Not only had they taken charge of their destiny, they had met two new friends. Though Luna knew they were not yet out of danger's way, she was finally able to rest.

chapter nineteen
FREEDOM'S FEAST

Luna woke at the first inkling of dawn.

As soon as the others stirred, she stood up and said, "We have to go."

Chief and Charlie rose onto their paws and stretched their legs without saying a word.

"You're leaving?" Jackson asked, rubbing his eyes.

"We just got to know you," added Jack. "What's the rush?"

"I want to go home," Luna said. Suddenly she realized how much she missed her mother.

Chief barked in agreement. "Me too."

Charlie was silent.

"What's wrong?" Chief asked, giving Charlie a companionable head bump.

"Nothing," said Charlie.

Luna walked over to him.

"What is it?" she asked.

Charlie covered his face with his paw.

"Nothing," he insisted.

Then Luna understood. Charlie didn't have a home to go to.

"There's plenty of room on Mr. Thomas's farm for all of us," she said. "You can meet Mother and Penny the chicken."

Charlie looked at her gratefully.

"Let's go," said Luna.

Jackson let loose a high-pitched trill.

"Are you crying?" asked Jack.

"No!" the chipmunk said indignantly. "I just got something in my throat."

Before they could go on, Luna walked over and nuzzled the chipmunks in thanks. Charlie and Chief did the same.

For once, Jack and Jackson didn't have anything to say. They led their guests to the tunnel's opening and out to the road. They listened and looked to make sure the way was clear. Then, cheek to cheek, they stood and watched as the puppies headed off for destinations unknown.

Gone was the exhilaration that had propelled Luna away from Puppy Paradise. But gone too was the terror. She no longer feared the worst because she had *experienced* the worst—or something close to it.

The three dogs trotted down the road looking purposeful, as if they knew how to get back to Mr. Thomas's farm. Fueled by food and by the kindness shown them by Jack and Jackson, they were determined to keep moving.

When Charlie asked Luna and Chief which path they were planning to take, Luna answered first. "We'll know when we get there."

Chief nodded. He didn't have a better answer.

Few cars traveled this lonely country road. Once in a while the ground rumbled, meaning a vehicle was approaching, the signal for them to hide behind trees or under bushes. They were taking no chances.

As the days passed, they became skilled at sneaking into barns to scavenge for food, filching animal feed, apples, potatoes, whatever they could find. They learned to follow the footprints of other animals that would lead them to ponds and streams.

One day while foraging in a barn, they stumbled onto a nest of chicks.

Charlie and Chief growled at the small yellow birds and said, "Let's eat them."

But Luna stepped between them and the nest.

"You can't do that," she said. "They're like the chicks back home."

Their debate was interrupted by the loud clucking of a hen. She kept her distance, furiously beating her wings.

"Why doesn't she come closer like crazy old Penny used to?" Luna asked Chief.

He looked at her and the hen and back again.

"We're a lot bigger than we were then," he said. "She must be scared."

None of them had noticed, but day by day they had grown. Charlie turned to Luna and asked, "Well? Should we eat them?"

Luna hesitated, pulled in one direction by instinct and another by the memory of Penny. Her stomach was rooting for instinct.

Just as she was about to decide, her dilemma was solved by a breeze carrying a whiff of something delightful. She forgot about the chicks and trotted toward the tantalizing smell. The fragrance drew her out the barn door, up a path, and to a farmhouse whose back door was ajar.

She nosed open the door. It was dark inside. No one seemed to be home.

The smell got stronger.

When Luna saw what she smelled, she barked, signaling the others to join her.

Whoever lived there had left a giant roast lamb cooling on the stove, and two pies on the table, one overflowing with blackberries, the other with cherries and peaches. The flaky crusts looked and smelled rich and buttery.

Within seconds all of them were inside. Chief stood on his back legs, grabbed the roast with his teeth, and yanked it onto the floor. Luna and Charlie brought the pies crashing to the ground. Luna found a giant bag of chips that she emptied onto the floor.

They had no remorse whatsoever about gorging on this feast. For several minutes they produced a barrage of joyful noise as they slurped and chewed, swallowed and belched.

When there didn't appear to be a scrap or crumb left, Chief rolled onto his side and stared at his swollen belly in a happy stupor. Then he belched.

Luna found one last morsel of pie that had been

flung under a cabinet. She stared at it for a second, wondering if she could eat another bite. Yes she could, she decided, and gobbled it up.

She licked her lips and sighed and stretched.

She lay peacefully on the floor for a minute or two, and then lifted her head.

"Sorry, pals," she said with regret. "We have to go."

Chief and Charlie stared at her as though they didn't understand a word she'd said. They could barely move, they were so stuffed. Despite her words, Luna was in no better shape. When she tried to pull herself to her feet, she sank back to the floor, weighed down by meat, chips, and pie.

Just as she extended her legs for another glorious stretch, all three of them heard the sounds of a car or truck approaching.

Fear is a great motivator. The dogs jumped to their feet as if they'd just spent the last half hour preparing for a race, not cramming food down their throats. Without a second of hesitation, they sprinted—out the door and back onto the road, almost colliding with the car pulling into the farmhouse driveway.

"Hey," yelled the driver as she slammed on the brakes.

By the time the woman could get through the door

to her house and take in the wreckage they'd left behind, the dogs were on their way, heavier and happier than they had been since they'd left home.

Freedom was a fine thing, but nothing was as satisfying to a hungry dog as food. With their systems jolted by sugar, salt, and protein, Luna and her companions kept going until dark and then collapsed in a comfortable pile of dirt near the road's edge.

That night, exhausted by flight and weighted down by a full belly, Luna slept without dreaming.

chapter twenty

LUNA'S DANCE

W hy did we have to leave Jack and Jackson?"
Luna asked one afternoon, when she was especially weary of scrounging for food.

"Why bring that up now?" Chief retorted. They had
been traveling for weeks by then.

Luna sighed. "I know, I know," she said.

"You're trying to get back home," Charlie chimed
in.

They kept moving across the hard winter terrain,
sometimes venturing onto the road but mainly hiding
in the sparse cover of the woods, stripped by cold.

All of them, even Charlie, had gotten muscled from constant exercise. But they still looked ratty. Their fur was matted and their ribs poked more prominently against the surface of their skin. Their eyes had hardened. They'd become thieves and sneaks, good at invading barns and storage bins, where they foraged for grain. Despite their friendly encounter with the chipmunks, the former pets had become fierce hunters, quick to pounce on rabbits and other small creatures. They were dogs in the wild now.

Some days were spirit-crushing, when the frigid weather and perpetual search for food wore them down. There were nights when they couldn't rest, no matter how tightly they snuggled against one another. But there were also those days when the sun filtered into the gray woods and the air was brisk rather than raw. On those days Luna felt as though she were flying, impervious to the elements, oblivious to the clawing and cracking of the frozen brambles and dry limbs that scratched her legs and clung to her fur.

Chief set the pace.

"The number one rule," he repeated frequently, "is stay together. We're harder to break when we run in a pack."

"Don't worry," Luna always replied. "I have no intention of being out here by myself."

"You can say that again," Charlie would chime in.

But one day Luna fell behind the others, distracted by a melody that ran through her head. It was Gilbert's song about the moon. She didn't know why it popped into her head, but there it was. That memory sparked another and another, and soon she was thinking of Gilbert and Mutt and Mr. Thomas's farm. Those were heavy thoughts she usually tried to push away because they slowed her down.

After some time Luna realized she was alone. She was startled but not frightened the way she once would have been. She had grown woods-wise. She could spot the trail carved into the frozen grass by Chief's and Charlie's paws, and she began to run. She kept her nostrils flared, seeking her companions' familiar smell.

Soon enough, her nose caught a whiff of Chief and Charlie. The wind was picking up, forcing Luna to bend her head as she ran. Her feet moved to the rhythm of Chief's number one rule: Stay together. Stay together.

As their scent grew stronger, another smell crowded in. Luna didn't know what it was.

Then her senses were jolted by an unfamiliar medley of sounds, a strange combination of clacking, woofing, and snorting.

She heard familiar, frantic barks.

"Chief!" she barked. "Charlie!"

Though she felt she'd been running as fast as she could, somehow she found deep reserves that propelled her even faster.

Her ribs hurt from breathing so hard, but she had to reach them. She raced through a thicket of evergreen brush, and came to a full stop.

The two dogs were standing like statues, staring at an enormous creature encased in a mass of thick, black fur. Luna had heard about bears but never seen one before.

He seemed terrifying, with huge paws that looked like they could smash a dog's face in without effort. His back was arched, as though he was ready to pounce.

Yet he wasn't pouncing. He was making all those weird noises as he and the dogs stared into one another's eyes.

"What are you doing?" Luna asked.

Charlie growled, "What do you think we're doing?"

Chief added, "You have to stare at a bear or he'll overpower you."

160

"How do you know that?" Luna asked.

Chief said impatiently, "Not now, Luna!"

Luna inhaled deeply and smelled something familiar. It was fear. But it wasn't coming from Charlie or Chief. It was coming from the bear.

He was afraid of them!

Later, when Luna remembered the encounter, she couldn't explain why she did what she did. It just felt right.

She started to dance.

Without taking her eyes off the bear's face, she trotted toward him. She trotted backward, just the way Gilbert had taught her. She wiggled her butt and stood on her hind legs.

The bear stared back. His teeth clacked a little less. He stopped snorting.

Luna sang (or believed she was singing), in a soft voice, "There's the moon eating olives . . ."

The bear stopped making any sounds at all as he stared at her.

"You'd think he'd never heard a dog sing before," Charlie whispered to Chief.

The wisecrack was not a good idea. The bear lifted his massive paw and turned toward Charlie.

Luna sang a bit louder, to bring the bear's atten-

tion back to her. He hesitated, half turned in Charlie's direction.

Luna continued until the giant creature swung back around to watch Luna 's steady performance.

"I think he's just afraid," she sang.

Chief muttered, "He's afraid of us?"

Luna sang, "Yes, I think he's afraid of us."

When Luna stopped singing and dancing, the four of them stood in the woods, silently staring at one another. Then without a fuss, the bear slipped away, as light on his feet as a cat.

The dogs stayed still, waiting.

After a few minutes had passed, Charlie asked, "What just happened?"

"I'll tell you what happened," Chief replied. "Luna danced away a bear."

Their triumph over the creature was exhilarating. After he left, they trotted a distance before stopping to celebrate by nipping at each other's necks and playing, a luxury they hadn't indulged in for a long time. For a few minutes, they were youngsters again, able to believe that it was important to wrestle one another to the ground. They faked one another out; they tumbled; they forgot to worry.

But as they lay panting on the ground, fear returned.

"What if he had decided to attack instead of run away?" Charlie mused.

"Shhh," said Luna. "Don't even think about that."

"I'll tell you what would have happened," Chief said. "He was twice the size of all of us put together. Did you see those paws? He would have demolished us!"

Tired as he was, he scrambled to his feet. "Let's go," he said with his most commanding bark.

Luna and Charlie defied him silently, simply staying where they were, sprawled on the ground.

Chief upped the ante. "What if that giant thing returns with friends?" he asked.

Even though their bones felt like water, Luna and Charlie lurched upright.

When Chief began to move, they followed.

"Where are we going?" Luna asked.

Charlie replied, "Let's find a spot near the road to sleep tonight."

They often returned to the road, pulled by the unspoken hope that it would eventually lead them home.

chapter twenty-one

OUT OF THE WOODS

Circumstances change. One day's hopeful wish can become the next day's disaster. The dogs were reminded of that in the morning when they found themselves trapped inside a large net.

"This is my fault," barked Chief loudly as two people scooped them up and hoisted them inside two crates waiting in the back of a large van. "I forced us to sleep by the road. I'm a fool."

"You aren't a fool," Luna cried out, without hesitation. "You did the right thing, how could you know?"

Charlie collapsed into the silence of captivity, as though their days of freedom had never happened.

165

They didn't have time to argue or philosophize. Before they realized what was happening, their captors—a large man and a small woman—had climbed into the back of the van. The man opened Luna's crate and reached his hand toward her. She growled as fiercely as she could.

"Take it easy, girl," he said. "Sit."

Even though his voice was gentle, Luna began to tremble, despite her efforts to remain still. Her shaking became more violent, but she didn't budge as the man lifted one ear and then the other.

"Look at this!" he called out. "This dog has her name tattooed on her ear."

Luna couldn't help herself. She yanked her head away from his hands and then cowered, waiting for her punishment.

It didn't come.

Instead, she heard the man's voice grow even softer.

"Don't worry, girl," he whispered as he squatted so that his face was at the same level as hers. She kept her gaze looking downward, but sneaked a glance at his. She saw nothing there that was frightening.

"This one is called Luna," he called out to his companion.

"Luna?" said the woman. "That sounds familiar."

The man looked puzzled.

"It does," he said. Then he snapped his fingers. "Now I know where I heard that name," he said. "She's one of Raymond's. You know, Puppy Paradise Raymond."

"Is that possible?" the woman replied. "We're miles and miles from there. You really think she could be Raymond's?"

The sound of that hated name chilled Luna. But she was calmed a bit by the way the man and woman both said it—Raymond—with irritation, the way Gilbert used to exclaim when he'd been bitten by a mosquito.

Was she imagining it, or were these people different?

"Here, Luna," the man said, holding out a dog biscuit. "You must be hungry."

Despite the signs that this man wasn't threatening, the treat put Luna back at Raymond's. Fear swept through her, making her feel she was being tested, knowing that if she lunged for the biscuit, she risked finding herself trapped in Hades' jaws. She willed herself to stop shaking and sat motionless, staring at the bottom of the crate.

"Look at this, Dr. Suzy," the man said in surprise.

Dr. Suzy looked up and said with a sigh, "I know, Bill. They're all afraid to eat."

Bill inspected their ears, dog by dog, and wrote their names in a notebook before scooting into the driver's seat.

"Don't worry," Dr. Suzy said to the dogs in a clear, calm voice. "You are going to be fine now. You don't have to run anymore."

None of them budged, but they were listening intently.

"Why should they believe me?" the woman said as she slid into the passenger seat. "That man should be arrested."

"Maybe he will be this time," Luna heard Bill say. "Finally someone who worked for him is willing to speak out. We've been hearing about him for years but have never been able to pin anything on him."

"I couldn't believe it," said Dr. Suzy, "when you told me about the young guy interviewed on the radio. The one who worked for him."

They hit a bump in the road, and Bill called out to the dogs, "You okay back there?"

Luna tried to focus on what the humans were saying.

"Why did Louis decide to blow the whistle on Raymond?" Dr. Suzy asked.

Bill explained. "It was actually these three!" he said. "When they made a break for it, Louis realized how miserable they must be. Their courage inspired him to tell the truth about Puppy Paradise. He went straight to the police with a full report, complete with pictures he'd taken."

"Did you hear that?" Luna asked Chief.

Chief nodded sleepily.

"Where do you think they're taking us?" Luna asked.

There was no answer. She saw that both Chief and Charlie had drifted off. Soon Luna followed them into a kind of half-sleep, her exhaustion overcoming her uncertainty.

Luna and the others woke up as the van was slowing to a stop.

They had arrived at a bright yellow building. Dr. Suzy and Bill slipped collars onto each of the dogs and snapped on a leash. This was something new, but the humans were so matter-of-fact about it that Luna and the other two dogs didn't object, and allowed themselves to be led inside.

Luna noticed that the yard was dotted with crocuses, just beginning to bloom. Winter was over.

chapter twenty-two

SECOND CHANCES

Welcome to Second Chances," Dr. Suzy said.

Luna gave a quick look around. The main room wasn't much, just some chairs, and a woman sitting behind a desk.

Dr. Suzy handed Luna's leash to Bill, who was holding on to Chief and Charlie. "Could you take our new guests out back while I catch up here?" she asked.

The three dogs followed Bill without making a sound, not knowing what to expect. When they walked through the door, Luna couldn't help but wag her tails at the delightful sight that greeted her. Dogs of all shapes and sizes roamed free in a room filled with old sofas and all kinds of toys. The dogs were neatly groomed and well behaved, eyeing the newcomers with curiosity but without commotion.

Suddenly Luna felt overwhelmed. She began to tug on her leash, trying to find somewhere to hide.

Bill knelt down and petted her.

"I know, it's a lot to take in, girl," he said. "Come with me."

Charlie and Chief began to whimper.

"You too, boys," Bill said in a kind voice.

He led the friends to yet another room, where several big cages were spread around, with plenty of space between them, each cage occupied by one dog. It was very clean. The animals in this room barked out weak greetings, and it was obvious that they were less robust, more timid, than the dogs out front.

Luna, Charlie, and Chief didn't make eye contact with any of them. After Puppy Paradise, they were wary of other dogs. Bill seemed to understand their need for privacy. He led the group to cages arranged in a cluster near one another. But these cages were nothing like the prisons that had confined them at Raymond's. These were large and clean, with solid bottoms, not wire floors that cut into their paws. Each cage contained a chew toy and a pillow, and the doors

were unlocked. They could walk out if they wanted to.

Charlie immediately grabbed his toy between his teeth, but Luna and Chief ignored theirs. They didn't have things like that back on the farm. It meant nothing to them.

At the beginning, they did little else besides sleep. They were exhausted, far more than they realized. They'd quickly run off that huge meal at the farmhouse. All three of them were bony, their coats dull and hanging on their frames.

It took some time for Luna to realize how awful they looked. Out in the wild, she had come to see Charlie as a hero. In her eyes, his fur had no longer seemed scraggly but instead wild and commanding. In their new peaceful surroundings, Charlie looked scrawny and weak, even pathetic.

All of them fell sick shortly after they arrived.

Dr. Suzy examined them.

"Just as I suspected," she told Bill. "They all have worms."

Luna's ears perked up. "Worms!"

Chief told her these were a different kind of worms, but she didn't care. The worms, whatever kind they were, just reminded her of how much she missed her mother, Gilbert, and the farm. She fell asleep whimpering with sorrow, remembering the day she had told Mutt that she was afraid of worms and her mother had teased her out of it. It seemed very long ago.

Days passed and she barely moved, weakened by the worms that had invaded her stomach. To Luna's disappointment and shock, she was almost as miserable as she had been at Raymond's Puppy Paradise. Someday she would come to realize that it made sense: For weeks she had lived in fear—fear of being beaten, fear of humiliation, fear of being scapegoat for a day. For weeks her constant companions had been filth, hunger, and dread—and the desire to escape. That desire had been a powerful motivation. Now it was gone.

Luna and the other two no longer needed to do their nightly exercises, or to buck one another up. They had lost purpose. Now they didn't feel like doing anything at all. So even though they weren't trapped inside their crates, they never ventured outside except when Dr. Suzy and Bill took them for fresh air.

One day Luna overheard Bill and Dr. Suzy talking about them.

"Is something seriously wrong?" Bill asked.

Dr. Suzy didn't answer right away.

"Physically they're getting better every day," she said. "But I think they are depressed."

"Should we be doing something else?" Bill asked.

Dr. Suzy shook her head.

"I've seen this many times," she said, "especially in brave animals like this bunch. Sometimes it's the ones with the most guts that have a hard time when they're rescued. It's like they've used up more than they had, and now they have to build themselves back to the starting point, where they feel like living again."

Luna was upset. She knew she should feel happy to be with these kind people, but instead she just felt limp, as if the spirit had been drained out of her. Would she ever care about anything again? She couldn't see how.

Then Bill asked the question that was always on her mind.

"What do you think will happen to them?" he asked.

Dr. Suzy walked over to Luna with a strange look on her face.

"Honestly?" the vet replied. "I believe they are going to be fine, but I can't lie and tell you why or how. Some dogs are survivors and some aren't. This bunch? They definitely are."

Hearing Dr. Suzy call them survivors was the first moment Luna began to feel safe.

chapter twenty-three

CHARLIE'S TURN

L una stared listlessly at the television set playing at low volume. It didn't interest her at all.

Charlie, however, was fascinated by the voices and the flashes of light and shadow that came from the box. He told Luna and Chief that it brought back memories of his owners, who had spent a great deal of time staring at the TV, with Charlie nestled on their laps.

The television meant nothing to Luna and her brother. There hadn't been one at Gilbert's house. Besides, there had been no extra time for him and his family to sit around; their shack hadn't been built for lounging.

One day Luna asked Charlie, "What do you find so interesting about it?"

He didn't take his eyes off the screen.

"I don't know," he said. "It's fun!"

Luna looked at him and then realized that Charlie had changed since they'd gotten to the shelter. If someone asked her to describe him now, she'd say he was cute!

His shaggy fur was clean and fluffed up; his eyes were bright and alert, peeping out from the curls that flopped onto them. His stomach had filled out just enough to make him look sturdy. For the first time since she'd met him, Charlie's looks matched his good-natured personality.

Luna soon realized she wasn't the only one who had noticed the transformation. The people running the shelter moved Charlie to the other part of the building, to be with the dogs who had recovered from whatever trauma had brought them there.

He didn't disappear. Not at all. All of the dogs gathered together in the yard most days, and Charlie would wander over to Luna and Chief to say hello. But he was disappearing in another way. While Luna and her brother remained in a strange state of numbness, Charlie had regained his spirit. He was always chasing a ball, or nipping at someone to get them to play with him. It was as if nothing bad had ever happened to him.

Luna envied him, but she was also glad.

"Someone is going to adopt you any minute," she said to her friend one day.

"I agree!" Charlie said happily. "That goes for all of us!"

But Chief and Luna were doubtful.

"What's wrong with us?" Luna asked her brother when Charlie had run off to play with someone else. "No one wanted us back at Mr. Thomas's. No one's going to want us now."

"That's not true," Chief said.

"Oh, yeah?" said Luna. "Where are Happy and Alegre?"

It was the first time she'd spoken their names in a long time.

"You know where they are," said Chief. "They were adopted."

Luna felt tired. "Yes," she said. "That's exactly what I mean."

She didn't realize that Charlie had rejoined them.

"I don't get it," he interjected. "Until the two of you

179

arrived I had completely given up. But now the tables are turned and I can't make you feel better."

He shook his head sadly. "Why?" he asked.

Luna was touched by her shaggy friend's sweetness.

"You do make us feel better, Charlie," she said. "You really do."

Soon, just as Luna predicted, a family came to take Charlie home with them. When that day arrived, Charlie barked at Luna.

"Could you do your little dance for me, one last time?" he asked.

Luna started to shake her head. She just didn't feel like it.

Chief chimed in. "Come on, Luna," he barked.

Chief began to walk forward and backward, a clumsy version of Luna's dance.

As she watched her brother, something shifted inside her. Before she knew what was happening, she felt herself smile.

And then she trotted over to Chief and gave him a playful nudge.

"Not like that, silly," she barked.

"Oh, yeah?" he asked. "Then how?"

"Like this," Luna said, and proceeded to show him. Her dance was the same but different. Before, Luna

had moved with the carefree joy of a puppy. Now each step she took carried the weight of everything that had happened to her.

"That is beautiful," Chief said, his voice full of admiration.

"Thank you," Charlie added.

"You are welcome," replied Luna. Then, without realizing she was doing it, she gave a little bow, just as Gilbert had taught her.

They were joined by Dr. Suzy and Charlie's new owner, a boy with shaggy hair just like Charlie's. The boy and dog looked as though they were made for each other.

"I have to go," Charlie said as the boy stood quietly by his side. He gently placed his forehead against Chief's and then Luna's.

"I will never forget you," Charlie said.

It took all of Luna's strength to nuzzle her friend in farewell. Though she was much stronger than she had been, she didn't know how many more times she could stand to be separated from someone she loved.

Chief and Luna sat down next to each other and silently watched Charlie trot out the door. Before he disappeared, he gave one quick glance backward, but Luna could tell from the eager way he wagged his tail that Charlie was ready to begin his new life.

chapter twenty-four

MARTY THE MAGICIAN

A fter Charlie left, Luna felt Dr. Suzy's eyes on her.
"Luna, come here," the vet said briskly. Luna
wanted to trust this kind person but she felt
she had forgotten how. She walked over and stood
next to Dr. Suzy, but stiffly, without moving a muscle,
and without looking at her.

Dr. Suzy laughed and knelt down.

"You will never beg for love, will you, girl?" she
asked as she pet Luna, who was surprised to find herself responding to the vet's gentle touch.

"Your brother is the same, isn't he?" Dr. Suzy continued.

As she scratched Luna's ears, Dr. Suzy began to hum.

The song she was humming reminded Luna of Gilbert's song. Without meaning to, she felt her paws start to move, and the movement felt good.

Dr. Suzy said with delight in her voice, "Luna! You know how to dance!"

When Luna heard the word "dance," she began to show off some fancy moves she'd forgotten she knew. As she twirled around, she was able to shake away the terrible memories she'd been carrying around.

When she heard Dr. Suzy clap, Luna felt happy.

"That was great!" Dr. Suzy said with a laugh. "Take a bow."

Luna was more than ready to take her bow.

"I've just seen the most remarkable thing," Dr. Suzy called out to Bill, who was in the other room.

A minute later he was by her side.

"What was it?" he asked.

"Luna knows how to dance," Dr. Suzy said. "And she knows what it means to 'bow.'"

"Really?" said Bill skeptically, wrinkling his forehead. "Luna knows how to dance? Are you sure she wasn't just stretching her legs?"

Dr. Suzy shook her head.

"Watch," she said, and asked Luna to dance again.

Luna didn't have to be asked twice. As she danced, she felt as though she had found a part of herself that had been lost. *If only Gilbert could see me,* she thought as she bowed again.

Dr. Suzy was grinning.

"There, you see?" she said.

Bill scratched his head. "I do see."

Luna could feel how pleased they were. She raised her paw in a friendly gesture.

Grasping the dog's paw, Dr. Suzy said to Bill, "Do you remember me telling you about my old friend Marty the dog trainer?"

For a few seconds Bill looked puzzled, and then he brightened. "Are you thinking what I think you are?"

Dr. Suzy nodded. "Exactly."

Luna didn't understand what they were talking about but she didn't care. She was just happy that she felt like dancing again.

"Excuse me, Luna," Dr. Suzy said, giving the dog one more scratch behind the ears. "I have to make a phone call."

A few days later a large man with a beard and light green eyes appeared at the shelter. He almost skipped through the door, as though he were really eager to get somewhere. Though he mumbled a greeting and nodded at Dr. Suzy, he didn't pause, just kept going, with the focus and purpose of a hunting dog.

"Nice to see you, Marty," Dr. Suzy said, but he didn't answer. Luna noticed that he ignored the puppies who sashayed and cuddled and struck adorable poses to get his attention. He noticed Luna, though. In fact, he seemed to have come just for her.

"That's Luna," called out Dr. Suzy.

"I can see that," he said, looking at Luna's face.

Then Dr. Suzy added a warning. "She doesn't like strangers."

The man didn't answer. With an intent look on his face, he dropped to his knees and gently laid his forefinger on the crescent moon above Luna's eye.

"Luna, what are you thinking?" he asked.

Normally, Luna's response to a stranger's touch would have been to freeze. Her instincts remained on high alert, despite the kind treatment she'd received at Second Chances. Puppy Paradise had left its imprint on her soul, not just on her ear.

But she trusted this man. He was big but light on

his feet, as if he were dancing across the floor. Luna had noticed that none of the other dogs showed the slightest bit of fear as the stranger approached. Even the most timid ones began to thump their tails, like a round of applause.

Still, Luna surprised herself when, without thinking about it, she rolled over on her back and stretched out, hoping he would pat her on the tummy.

"You are a magician!" Dr. Suzy said, admiration in her voice. "She's never done that before."

The man didn't take his eyes off Luna.

"That's what they call me," he said. "Marty the Magician."

He reached into the small bag slung over his shoulder and pulled out a treat.

Luna didn't hesitate. She sat up and clamped her teeth on the biscuit.

Chief walked over to see what was going on.

"Why do you look so surprised?" Luna asked him, chewing contentedly.

Chief shook his head. "I thought you weren't ever going to be yourself again," he said.

"Well, here I am," Luna said with a grin. "And I just had a treat and you didn't!" Being around Marty made her feel frisky, like it was okay to have fun.

She was glad when she heard the man say to Dr. Suzy, "Give me some time with them."

Dr. Suzy led him to a large empty room, and motioned Luna and Chief to join them.

Soon Marty was instructing, yelling, praising, whispering, and laughing. Luna and Chief fixed their eyes on his, waiting for his next signal with anticipation. Luna discovered she already knew most of his commands: Sit! Stand! Relax!

From the get-go, she understood that Marty wasn't anything like Raymond. There wasn't a whiff of cruelty about him. He was more like Gilbert, who expected a lot of her because he believed in her. Obeying Marty felt like coming home, at least a little.

When it was time to rest, Marty sat next to them on the floor, scratching their bellies and talking to them in a gentle voice.

"Okay," he said after a few minutes. "It's time."

When Marty stood up, the dogs followed him into Dr. Suzy's office. "What happened in there?" she asked Marty. "They look like different dogs."

"Basic training," he said, and turned to give Luna and Chief a wink.

"Could you elaborate?" she asked impatiently.

He laughed.

"No trick to it," he said. "They're smart dogs, these two. All they needed was someone to help them remember what they already knew."

Dr. Suzy nodded.

"Well," she said. "What do you think?"

Marty looked at her. His face didn't offer any clues.

He stood there for a while, staring at Luna and Chief, who were quietly desperate to hear what he would say.

Finally, he responded.

"I'll take them," he said.

Luna's tail began thumping with a happiness she couldn't explain. Chief joined in.

"Just like that?" Dr. Suzy said with surprise.

"Just like what?" Marty responded.

A few minutes later, he led the dogs outside, opened the back door of his car, and pointed inside. Chief hopped in, but Luna felt it was okay to disobey Marty this one time. She ran back to Dr. Suzy and lifted her paw to say good-bye. Then she was ready to go. She returned to the car and joined Chief in the backseat. As she dozed off to the rhythm of the car's steady motion, she dreamed of Mutt. How she wished her mother knew that her puppies had figured out how to be brave, just the way she said they would.

chapter twenty-five

DOGS IN THE CITY

They soon discovered that while Marty wasn't much of a talker, he loved to sing, just like Gilbert. He serenaded them for mile after mile. He didn't mind if they howled along, and wasn't insulted if they took a nap instead.

Time passed pleasantly. Marty's car was very old and quite large, with spacious windows that allowed a lot of sunlight to filter in. The seats became nice and warm, a lovely place to curl up and nod off.

For the first time since she'd left the farm, Luna didn't feel as though she were in limbo, even though she had no idea what lay ahead. She was satisfied just to exist, to be with Chief and this odd, appealing man. Marty gave her the feeling that she was traveling with a purpose.

They stopped whenever Marty got hungry or saw something by the edge of the road that he felt required a closer look. During these breaks, he offered the dogs a few pointers on how to respond to commands. They sat. They relaxed. They rolled over. He began teaching them to pivot and to crawl.

Sometimes Marty drove very fast, which caused the countryside rushing by to melt together into a blurry impression of colors. The dogs loved these stretches, when the wind blew their fur back. Marty always kept the windows rolled down. At other times he drove very slowly, allowing the dogs to take in the changing landscape as it drifted by.

"He's unpredictable," observed Luna, after several hours had passed.

"That's true," agreed Chief. "But I don't find him threatening or nerve-wracking, do you?'

"Not at all," Luna agreed.

Eventually the scenery changed from green to gray. The dogs pressed their faces against the window to look.

"What are those things?" Luna asked Chief.

He was trying to figure it out when Marty announced, "This, my furry friends, is the big city, your new home."

"What's a city?" Chief asked.

Luna replied, "You've heard about them on those shows Charlie used to watch on television. They're just places where a lot of people live close together." Then she added, "I wonder what it will be like there."

Chief tried not to sound worried, though Luna wasn't convinced. "Marty wouldn't take us somewhere that wasn't good," he said.

Now they were driving much more slowly in fits and starts. They were surrounded by cars, buses, bicycles, trucks, and more people than they had imagined could exist.

"Look!" barked Luna. "A dog!"

The dog nodded at her and then walked away, pulling his owner with him.

The car stopped.

"You two have brought me luck!" exclaimed Marty. "We found a parking spot right in front of my building."

Luna didn't know what he was talking about, but it seemed to make him happy.

Marty stepped outside, stretched his arms in the

air, and stomped his feet on the ground. Then he opened the back door so the dogs could jump out.

They copied him by stretching their legs and stomping their paws on the ground.

Then they sat and looked at Marty expectantly.

Before he could say a word, a loud voice startled them.

"IS THAT MARTY THE SO-CALLED MAGICIAN NOT PAYING ATTENTION TO HIS ANIMALS?"

The dogs didn't move.

A skinny man with a long white beard was walking toward them.

"What's *wrong* with you?" he yelled at Marty.

Chief put a paw on Luna's back. She was glad, because she was feeling nervous. She noticed that Chief was also keeping his eyes on the ground. Neither of them moved a muscle.

"Those dogs could run out into traffic and get hurt!" the man yelled at Marty. "What are you thinking?"

Marty ignored him and knelt down next to the dogs.

"Well, my friends," he said with a grin, "welcome to New York."

The dogs remained frozen in place. Marty, however, stood up and headed directly toward the white-haired man and gave him a hug.

"Hey, Izzy," he said. "Don't you have anything better to do than lecture me?"

Luna was afraid to look. Was Marty just as crazy as that man? What was he thinking? Had he saved them just to end up in trouble himself?

"Look at that," Chief whispered.

Izzy was chuckling and talking to Marty in a normal tone.

Luna couldn't catch what they were saying to each other, but it was obvious that they were friends. Soon Izzy turned and walked away, shaking his head.

"He's got his own way of looking at things," Marty said as pulled his knapsack out of the car. "He worries about everything."

"Why are humans so weird?" Luna asked Chief.

"I don't know," Chief said. "But Marty is cool."

"Agreed," said Luna. She nodded, but her body remained wary. The excitement she had been feeling was replaced by uncertainty.

Without looking at them, Marty walked up to the closest building and put his key in the front door. He looked over his shoulder.

"Well?" he said. "What are you waiting for?"

"Does he think we know what to do?" Luna said to Chief, feeling annoyed. "We don't even know where we are or why we're here."

Chief said gently, "I think he just wants us to come inside."

Luna responded, "I know that, but I'm tired. I want to go home."

Chief seemed to understand. "Me too," he said.

As they communicated in low growls, Luna felt Marty looking at them.

"Poor things," Marty muttered, but he didn't budge from the doorstep.

When Luna and Chief didn't move, he asked them again, "What are you waiting for?"

With that, he walked inside, leaving the door open.

Luna sighed.

"Come on," she said to her brother. "What else can we do?"

chapter twenty-six

FITTING IN

Their first days in the city didn't put Luna's unease to rest. She was accustomed to sniffing things out, but in New York there were so many smells and sounds, it was hard to tell one thing from another. Everything was loud, fast, big.

Marty had them dive right in. They barely had time to walk around his giant loft before he'd hitched them to leashes and plunged them into the fray. Things that city dogs took for granted were alien to them. Fire hydrants, bus stops, police sirens, pizza: They had encountered none of these things in the Pennsylvania countryside.

Things that were familiar were unfamiliar—city dogs, for example. They pranced next to their owners like royalty, casting disdainful looks at the country bumpkins. Or that's what it felt like to Luna.

But it didn't take long for her to see the city's strange beauty. Marty took them for nighttime prowls in parks, where they could run without their leashes, with light provided by lamps rather than the moon. There they could inhale the smell of grass and trees, roll in dirt, race each other until their hearts pounded with exhaustion and happiness.

Luna and Chief became accustomed to having people stop Marty to discuss them. "Are they related to each other?" "I love your dogs!" "Can I pet them?"

They made the acquaintance of some neighborhood dogs and learned to avoid the local bullies.

Even Izzy became their friend, always sneaking them a treat when he saw them. They discovered that he was just one of a large cast of characters who seemed to know Marty. Elegant women dressed in stylish clothes waved and said, "Hi, Marty." Firefighters and police officers seemed to know who he was.

They learned that he was called Marty the Magician because he was the most respected dog agent in the business, known for his astute judgment and his unconventional methods.

Marty explained his philosophy to them one day. "I like to work on my own terms," he said. "I am just as interested in providing service dogs to people who need them as I am in finding the next movie star dog."

Luna and Chief were too busy being tourists in New York to worry about what Marty's job actually was.

Then one day Marty said to them, "It's time to get to work."

"Work" turned out to be no different than play. Marty's home was like an indoor park. He'd carved out a tiny bedroom for himself; the rest was open space dedicated to training. There were a big over-stuffed couch, a big television, and lots of tables and chairs scattered around. There were a stove and a refrigerator, which contained raw meat for the dogs and not much else.

The floor was made out of a variety of surfaces: wood, carpet, stone, and tile.

And there were many places to hide. Marty had rigged tents of various sizes and plopped them down in no special pattern.

It was an odd abode for a human but delightful for

dogs. It didn't hurt that Marty believed treats weren't reserved for rewards. Sometimes he just handed one out for fun.

On their first day of "work," Marty just kept tossing toys at them, then hiding them in different tents.

From the moment Marty threw a rag doll across the room, Chief loved the game. Luna could tell that the sport drove everything else from his mind. Nothing could distract him from his goal of tracking down every single ball, squeeze toy, fake bone, and piece of rope that Marty had hidden. Chief was relentless.

Luna was more reluctant to play along—even when Marty tossed a hollow toy that he'd spiced with dollops of peanut butter. Puppy Paradise had taught her too well: Wait. Watch. Don't give in to desire.

It wasn't that she didn't trust Marty; she just trusted him differently than Chief did. Chief had decided to trust without reservation. If Marty wanted to play, he would play.

Luna waited for instructions. When Marty ordered them to fetch, she fetched. If he didn't, she waited.

Marty didn't yell or scold. He watched and made notes in a small journal that he kept tucked in his back pocket.

They proceeded from chasing toys on command, to jumping on chairs, to wrestling with Marty on the wood floor, the ceramic tile, the stone. He timed how long they would battle him when he tried to pull a toy from their mouths.

Sometimes while Chief rested, Marty turned his full attention to Luna. He played all kinds of music for her and taught her many new dance steps. Luna loved dancing with Marty. He was an excellent partner. No matter how fancy his footwork, she kept up— and added a few flourishes of her own.

When Marty took them outdoors for walks, he paid special attention when strangers approached them, and was always jotting things in his notebook.

Just as Marty was watching them, the dogs were watching him too.

One day Luna said to Chief, "Do you think Marty has a plan for us or does he just like to play?"

"He must have a plan," Chief said. "Grown humans never just play."

When Marty wasn't observing the dogs, he was talking on the phone, writing in his notebook while he talked. Every so often, he snapped photographs of them. Sometimes he put on fancy clothes and was picked up in front of the building by a black limousine. They watched from the window, curious.

A woman Marty called Sarge dropped by one afternoon. He proudly showed her what Chief and Luna had learned. The dogs retrieved keys when he dropped them on purpose. Then he unfolded a wheelchair that he kept in the apartment, and they moved alongside him as he wheeled around the room. When he tried to scare them by yelling at them for no apparent reason, neither Luna nor Chief reacted. They waited patiently, just as Marty had taught them.

For several visits Sarge watched without comment. Then one day, without warning, she pulled a whistle out of her pocket and put it in her mouth, producing an ear-splitting shriek.

The piercing noise stopped Luna in her tracks. She stood shaking with fear.

Chief was in pursuit of a missing toy; the searing sound didn't faze him. In fact, he barely blinked, as if nothing out of the ordinary had happened.

"See what I mean?" Marty said to Sarge as she watched Chief closely.

The woman nodded.

"He looks good," she said. "I think he's ready."

Marty called Chief over.

"Chief, my boy," he said in a formal voice, "you are going to live up to your name. Sarge here agrees with me that you have what it takes to become a police dog. You are dedicated, unswerving, friendly, and tough."

Marty's words made Chief straighten up with pride.

Luna felt proud too. She walked over to her brother, and said, "I always knew you would do something important."

Though her words were true, saying them made Luna's heart ache. From the minute she was born, she had counted on Chief. He was her companion in every way. Only Chief knew where she had come from and everything she had endured. Only Chief knew what Mutt's promise had meant to both of them. She was happy that he had found his promise, but would she ever find hers? And now she would have to say good-bye to him too.

Chief pressed his head against his sister's. No words were needed to express how they felt about each other.

This bittersweet moment was interrupted by Marty's voice.

"Luna, come here," he said. "I have some news for you too."

chapter twenty-seven

WORKING DOGS

Luna became a dog for hire. She appeared in advertisements, television shows, and at charity events. All the lessons she had learned—the positive ones from Gilbert and negative ones from Raymond—had prepared her for work that required patience and obedience. She never missed a cue and had no trouble pretending to like strange children who petted her. Sometimes she was asked to dance, and she did that too, without making a fuss. It turned out that shy Luna was a natural performer.

Marty wasn't just an excellent trainer, he was a good promoter. Often when he talked to people about hiring Luna, she would hear him tell them about her escape from Raymond's—her heroic tale. One day a local news station even did a story about her and Chief. The gentle reporter, with tears in his eyes, exclaimed, "You have never seen dogs this smart, or noble. What natural talent!"

Looking into the camera, the reporter speculated on who their mother might have been. "Clearly, she must have been a dog of fine pedigree," he said. "It is quite amazing for dogs so young to have endured and accomplished so much. Just over a year old, they have experienced more than many dogs do in a lifetime."

Luna tried to feel contented. She was glad that Chief was happy. Sarge had matched him with a kind, quiet policeman named Mike who belonged to the K-9 unit. Their job was to help rescue people who were trapped in rubble when buildings fell down because of construction accidents or explosions. Mike never failed to treat Chief with respect. They worked together and lived together. Mike welcomed Chief into his family. The two of them traveled together all over the city, trying to make sure it was a safe place.

Marty had made a deal with Sarge that Chief and Luna would be able to see each other regularly. Mike kept the bargain, and every week he and Marty brought the dogs together, usually in a park where they could run and play.

On one of those afternoons, Luna said to her brother, "You have found a home, haven't you, Chief?"

When he nodded, she said softly, "I wish our mother could see you."

Chief cocked his head and looked at his sister. He knew her as no one else could.

"And you, Luna?" he asked. "Are you happy?"

She sighed.

"I'm not unhappy," she replied.

"What is it?" Chief asked.

Luna blurted it out. "I don't want to complain, because I have so much," she said. "I would do anything for Marty. But I can't stay with him, because . . ."

She paused, but Chief prompted her. "Because why?"

Luna continued. "Because he *discovers* dogs; he doesn't adopt them," she said. "I heard him tell someone he's looking for a good place for me to live. Then when we were out for a walk I saw this sad-looking dog—he reminded me of Charlie when we first saw him. This poor dog was wearing a blanket on his back that said, 'Adopt Me.' Am I going to end up like him?"

Chief listened sympathetically.

Luna went on. "I felt like I hadn't come very far at all," she said. "All I wanted at that minute was to see our mother and Gilbert and even that crazy hen Penny. I wanted to see Charlie!"

Chief thought for a minute and then said, "Luna, remember how our mother told each of us that we were more like her than we know?"

Luna barked in amusement. "Yes, and I thought it was a special message just for me!" she said.

"Well, I think it was," said Chief. "You are Luna, Mutt's puppy. Everything will work out, you'll see."

Luna wasn't so sure, but she gave her brother a mischievous nip on the neck, the way they did when they were little.

"I hope you're right," she said as she trotted toward Marty.

Then she turned and gave him a sisterly bark.

"Hey, Chief," she called out, "I'm willing to believe you."

chapter twenty-eight

THE PERFORMANCE
OF A LIFETIME

In the weeks that followed, Luna worked hard.
Yet there was one event coming up that seemed
special to Marty. He pushed her hard, going
over and over dance steps and routines she could do
in her sleep.

The morning of that performance, as he brushed
her fur until it glistened, he told her about the worthy
cause she would be participating in. Then he rattled
off the list of famous people who would be appearing
onstage with her, right in the middle of Times Square.

"Just do what you always do," Marty said in a soothing voice.

Luna was perplexed. Why would she do anything else?

When a limousine picked them up at Marty's, Luna didn't blink. She had grown accustomed to riding in fancy cars. But when she stepped out of the car, at the edge of Times Square, Luna felt as disoriented as she did when she and Chief first arrived in New York. Though she had grown accustomed to crowds and commotion, she had never experienced a carnival like this. Marty kept up a calming stream of talk as they pushed their way through people walking, selling things, making pronouncements, and pointing at some marvel or another.

Soon they arrived at a stage that had been set up in the middle of the broad street. The sidewalk was crammed with children and adults holding notebooks and cameras, hoping to get autographs or have their pictures taken with the celebrities who were coming there to help raise money.

But the stage was empty except for people checking the microphone and making sure everything was where it was supposed to be.

Marty led Luna to a parked trailer. He laughed and pointed at the sign on the door.

"Look, girl," he said. "It says LUNA! You are a star now!"

Luna followed Marty up the stairs into the trailer. Inside, there was a small couch and a table that was holding a bottle of water, a basket of fruit, and a cup filled with dog treats. On the floor, Luna found a big bowl of water, which she appreciated. All of the hub-bub had made her nervous and thirsty.

She rested on the couch while Marty talked on the telephone. Luna couldn't tell how much time had passed when there was a knock on the door and someone called out, "You ready?"

Marty scratched Luna's ears.

"Okay, Luna," he said. "It's showtime."

The two of them peered out of the trailer window and watched an older man emerge from the trailer next to theirs. People started calling out his name and waving. He waved back and stopped to sign the papers they pushed in front of him as he made his way to the stage.

"That's the TV star," Marty said, chuckling.

Soon the man was followed by other people, including a teenage girl, a famous pop singer. When she walked through the door, everyone screamed and shouted.

"She's a pro," said Marty, with admiration in his voice. "Look, Luna, see how she just acts like nothing out of the ordinary is going on? That's what you have to do."

Marty pointed out a baseball player and a politician, and then he repeated, "It's showtime."

He pushed open the door, and Luna followed him. She kept her eyes on Marty, trying to ignore the mass of arms, legs, and bodies that pushed and shoved and shouted. She kept her head up and her gait even, just as Marty had told her to do.

Her dignified approach drew a wave of "Ooh" and "Ahh" and "Oh, isn't she cute!"

When Luna climbed the steps to the top of the stage, she turned to face the crowd, paused, and raised her paw, just the way Marty had taught her.

The crowd responded with chants of "Lu-na! Lu-na! Lu-na!"

Luna gazed ahead the way actors do, giving everyone the impression that she was looking at him or her, when actually she was straining to hear her cue.

Instead, through the noise, she thought she heard something familiar, a song she hadn't heard in a very long time.

"Allá está la luna, comiendo aceitunas . . ."

Luna's head jerked around and she began to bark.

Marty looked shocked. Nothing ever distracted Luna from her assigned task.

"What is it, girl?" he asked.

Through the chants and laughter of the crowd, the words came through even stronger. "*Yo le pedí una, no me quiso dar.*"

Luna began to dance, three steps one way, three steps back.

Then she stopped and gazed frantically out into the crowd, her ears on high alert.

"What's going on, Luna?" Marty asked.

Luna wasn't sure herself. Had she just imagined the song or was it real? She stood very still, with her ears as alert as they had ever been.

Then she heard what she was listening for.

"*Saqué el pañuelito, me puse a llorar.*"

That did it! Luna broke loose of her leash and pushed her way through the crowd.

"Look, the dog is running away!" called out a little girl with delight.

Luna ignored her and everything else. Nothing could stop her—not the crush of humanity trying to block her path, not even the sound of Marty's bewildered voice yelling, "Come back, Luna!" She kept

moving toward her destination, each step filled with love and hope.

They saw each other at the same time.

"Luna!" cried Gilbert. "Is that you? I *knew* it was you."

Luna stopped, but just long enough to catch her breath.

Then, keeping her eyes on Gilbert to make sure he was really there, she began to dance.

chapter twenty-nine

AND THEN . . .

G ilbert threw his arms around Luna, ignoring everyone, including Marty, who finally caught up with her.

"How did you get here?" Gilbert asked Luna, who responded by licking his face and panting with joy.

Marty saw this was no ordinary fan.

"Who are you?" he asked Gilbert, his voice wavering between suspicion and curiosity.

Before Gilbert could reply, his mother stepped between him and Marty.

"Who is asking?" she replied.

Marty, as usual, knew exactly what to do.

He extended his hand and bowed slightly, ignoring the crowd milling around them.

"I am Marty, Luna's trainer," he said. "A pleasure to meet you, Mrs. . . ."

Gilbert's mother was charmed, like almost everyone who met Marty.

Marty pointed to the trailer with Luna's name on it.

"Why don't we meet there after the show?" he suggested, as if nothing out of the ordinary had taken place.

"Meanwhile, young man," he said to Gilbert, "since Luna seems so fond of you, why don't you join us onstage while she performs, and then we'll find out what this is all about."

Gilbert glanced at his mother, who nodded.

This time when Luna mounted the steps to the stage, she felt as if she were flying. She looked out at the cheering crowd with a new sense of peace. For the first time, she felt the long journey away from Raymond had reached an end.

Afterward, Luna lay curled up at Gilbert's feet while the grown-ups talked and the boy chimed in.

"We lived on a farm," Gilbert's mother said.

"And there was a dog named Mutt, the best dog in the world," added Gilbert.

Luna lifted her head.

Gilbert laughed. "And then she had puppies who were the best puppies in the world."

Marty learned about Mr. Thomas and the chickens, and then he told Gilbert and Silvia what he knew about Puppy Paradise.

"A puppy mill!" Gilbert's eyes widened. "How did they get there? Mr. Thomas wouldn't do that. I don't believe it."

His mother looked sad. "I don't want to believe it either," she said. "But then he never wrote back to us . . ."

Marty shook his head.

"There's a lot we don't know," he said. "How did Luna and Chief end up there, and where did they get the strength to overcome circumstances that destroyed the spirit of so many other dogs?"

Gilbert responded eagerly.

"I know part of the answer," he said. "They're like Mutt." He told Marty the story of how Mutt protected Butch from the fisher cat, a story that now seemed ancient, a fable from long ago. Luna loved hearing it again.

Marty nodded. "That makes sense," he said.

He looked at Gilbert. "How did you know Luna would be here?" he asked.

Silvia explained. "We saw something about the

event on television and when Gilbert saw the mark above Luna's eye—"

"I thought she was Mutt!" Gilbert interrupted.

"And I said it couldn't be," continued Silvia, "and then they said her name was Luna."

"And we realized Luna would be big by now," Gilbert said. "So we came to see . . ."

His voice trailed off and he knelt down to wrap his arms around Luna.

Marty scratched Luna's head and then laid his hand on Gilbert's shoulder.

"I have a feeling you taught Luna to dance," Marty said.

Gilbert looked surprised.

"Are you a magician?" he asked. "How did you know?"

Marty smiled without answering.

"Gilbert," he said, "could you watch Luna while I talk to your mother for a few minutes?"

The two grown-ups went outside the trailer for quite a while, which suited Luna just fine. They could have left her there with Gilbert forever.

Gilbert pressed his cheek against Luna's fur and began to talk.

"Mutt was there for me when I was alone on the farm," he said. "And then she kind of gave you to me, to take care of the way she took care of me."

Luna sighed with happiness.

Gilbert laughed. "But I know we both took care of each other."

Then he sat up in alarm. Marty and Silvia were standing in front of them, and Luna saw that they looked very serious.

"Gilbert, it's time for me to go," said Marty.

"No!" said Gilbert. "Mama, he can't take Luna away now, don't let him."

"Gilbert, *mi pequeno*—" said his mother.

Gilbert interrupted. "I am not a little one, and I won't lose Luna again," he said angrily.

Luna couldn't believe what she was hearing. She began to bark.

"Luna, quiet!" said Marty in a firm voice. Then he grinned and looked at Gilbert. "We completely agree," he said.

Gilbert and Luna both turned to his mother.

She was smiling.

Marty picked up Luna's leash and held it out to Gilbert.

"Here," Marty said. "Your mother and I agree that Luna belongs with you, though there is one important condition."

As Gilbert stared at the leash, Luna shook her head,

unable to believe what she was hearing.

Gilbert looked at his mother. "Mama?" he asked.

She nodded.

Luna barked.

Silvia laughed and scratched Luna's neck.

"Yes, Luna," she said. "It's okay."

"What about Papa?" Gilbert asked.

His mother made a funny face. "What do you think, I wouldn't ask him?" she said in a teasing voice. "I called him while Marty and I were talking."

She reached over and took the leash from Marty, then handed it to Gilbert.

"What do you say, Gilbert?" his mother prodded.

"Is it true?" he asked Marty, who laughed.

"I meant, say thank you," said his mother, blushing.

Marty shook his head. "I owe Gilbert as many thanks as he owes me," he said graciously.

Then Gilbert remembered something Marty had just said.

"What do you mean by condition?" he asked, with a note of fear in his voice.

Marty smiled. "I don't think you'll mind," he said.

Gilbert listened intently.

So did Luna.

"Luna has a promise from me that she can see

Chief once a week or so," Marty said. "You will have to keep that promise on my behalf."

Gilbert shouted with relief. "Yes, I can keep that promise," he said almost before Marty had gotten the words out.

Gilbert hugged Luna.

"Yes!" he repeated.

Luna walked over to Marty full of gratitude. He had made Mutt's prediction come true. She had found her talent. She lifted her paw in thanks. She would never forget the magic he had performed, simply by believing in her.

"You are most welcome, Luna," he said, taking her paw in his hand. "Most welcome indeed."

chapter thirty

BACK WHERE
IT ALL BEGAN

Summer had passed uneventfully on Mr. Thomas's farm. The man who took Lorenzo's place had come alone, without a family. Whenever Mutt walked by his small house—the house where Gilbert had lived—her tail would start wagging, as though she expected the boy to walk out the door. Some days a shift in the wind caused her to poke her head in the crawl space and sniff around, trying to pick up a whiff of her puppies. She wasn't sad or anxious, but her memories had become mingled with her instincts. Remembering Gilbert and the puppies was now part of her routine.

She listened to Mr. Thomas blame himself for sending Luna and Chief to Puppy Paradise. She heard him agonize out loud over his failure to reply to the letters from Lorenzo and Gilbert.

At first, he kept making excuses.

"I'll wait until I have more information," he would tell himself, while Mutt was listening. "I don't even know where the puppies are now."

As months went by he tried to convince himself—and Mutt—that he didn't have a choice, it was too late to respond.

"What is the point?" he asked Mutt. "We'll never see one another again."

One day after supper he sat on the porch with Mutt and Butch, who often lay side by side. It had been a process, for both cat and man, but their grudging gratitude toward Mutt had morphed into affection. The three of them sat in companionable silence while Mr. Thomas read the newspaper.

He was idly turning the pages when his eyes settled on something.

"Look at this," he said to Mutt and Butch.

He showed them a photograph of two dogs, though Mutt couldn't make out who they were.

"Listen," Mr. Thomas said, his voice shaking with excitement.

Mutt sat up and listened as he began to read aloud.

"Lots of plays have riveting first acts, then fade away after intermission. But we are happy to report that one doggy drama has had a marvelous second act."

Mutt didn't find this very interesting and lay back down. But as Mr. Thomas continued, she sat back up.

"Luna is a protége of Marty the Magician, a well-known New York dog agent who provides animals for TV commercials, plays, movies, and events."

At the sound of the name Luna, Mutt's tail began to thump.

Mr. Thomas stopped reading to look at her. Mutt barked, urging him to continue.

Mr. Thomas went on.

"Not long ago, Luna attracted local attention when her story was featured on local newscasts. It was great human interest, about a dog who overcame hardship to become a working dog in the big city. The persevering pooch's story was all the more engaging because she had a brother, Chief, who shared her adventures and then became a local New York hero, a member of the elite K-9 corps of police dogs."

Mutt had never heard Mr. Thomas sound so happy.

"Mutt, can you believe this?" asked Mr. Thomas.

He continued reading the story to her. Mutt listened to the tale of how her puppies escaped from a puppy mill and then were taken in by a local animal shelter, where they were discovered by a man named Marty, a dog agent.

Mutt saw Mr. Thomas's eyes fill with tears as he read the next part.

"For many, the determination of these pups became inspirational. Where did they get the strength to overcome circumstances that destroyed the spirit of so many other dogs? Was it breeding or something else?"

His hands were shaking as he put down the newspaper.

"Did you hear that, Mutt?" Mr. Thomas asked. "They are just like you, chips off the old block!"

Mutt listened intently, full of pride and relief, as Mr. Thomas told her the rest of the story.

"You aren't going to believe this!" he said. "Luna and Chief found Gilbert! And Lorenzo's restaurant is doing well."

Mutt's tail began thumping even harder at the sound of her friends' names.

Mr. Thomas started laughing, a sound so loud and unexpected that even lazy old Butch the cat raised his head with a glimmer of interest.

"It's called Broadway Dogs and Tacos, specializing in Mexican and American fast food," he said. "What they won't think of next."

He shook his head in admiration. "That Lorenzo was always a smart fellow," he said as he continued reading.

A minute later he exclaimed again. "And listen! They've put your girl Luna on a billboard to advertise the place. Isn't that amazing?"

That evening Mutt watched Mr. Thomas put the newspaper article in a frame and hang it near the spot where Mutt liked to sleep in the living room. The next morning, he announced that he had written a letter to Gilbert's family.

"Mutt," he said as he sealed the envelope, "I think you and I will be taking a trip to New York pretty soon. What do you think of that?"

She held up her paw, which Mr. Thomas grasped in his hand for a quick shake. Though she felt like celebrating, she trotted toward the fields as she always did. She had a job to do.

Mutt kept up a calm and steady pace as always, but her heart was still galloping with pride when she bumped into Penny. The dog told her friend what she had learned about Luna and Chief's journey.

"I told my puppies, one by one, that they would find their talents," Mutt said. "But I confess, I didn't really know for certain. Sometimes a promise is a hope, not a prediction."

Penny nodded.

"It takes courage to trust in a promise," said the wise hen. "But are you surprised to hear what Luna and Chief have accomplished? After all, they are your puppies!"

THE END

AUTHOR'S NOTE

After the publication of our previous book *Cat in the City,* Jill Weber and I visited dozens of schools, libraries, and bookstores talking to kids. They always asked about the creative process. Where do ideas come from? Why did you choose these characters? How do you come up with the plot? What is it like to work as an author/illustrator team?

The idea for Mutt came to me after talking to my mom. She is an immigrant who lost everything during World War II, when she was young. She survived terrible things yet remained an optimistic person who makes everyone who meets her feel better. I've learned so much from her, yet always wondered if I could ever be as brave as she is.

About the characters: I grew up in a tiny town in Ohio, where my family had a dog we loved named Poochie. Almost every year Poochie gave birth to puppies. This was a huge event. Mutt, Luna, and the other puppies grew from these memories. Jill lives on a farm in New Hampshire with her dog Sadie and a new puppy named Lottie. We talk a lot about our dogs and their personalities.

The plot developed from one question: What would happen to puppies taken from a loving home and put into danger? How would they survive? Where does their courage come from?

My job is to write the story and then Jill shows me what I've written in pictures! It's exciting to see the characters in my head interpreted by such a talented artist. Though each of us has done many books alone or with other people, we love collaborating with each other. *Mutt's Promise* is our third joint production.

There's a lot more to say about all of this, but I've run out of room! Jill and I just hope you've enjoyed reading the book as much as we have enjoyed creating it.

—*Julie Salamon*

A NOTE ON PUPPY MILLS

Sadly, while Puppy Paradise is a fictional creation, puppy mills are very real—and too many dogs do not find happy endings. If you want to adopt a dog, it is important to work through reputable organizations. Please make sure the breeder or shelter you use has cared for your future pet with kindness and concern for its health.

Whether you are choosing a pet or simply care about animals, learn more from the many organizations working to protect them. These include:

American Society for the Prevention of Cruelty to Animals: ASPCA.org

The Humane Society: humanesociety.org

National Mill Dog Rescue: milldogrescue.org

North Shore Animal League America: animalleague.org

Hearts United for Animals: hua.org

ACKNOWLEDGEMENTS

At Dial, Nancy Conescu and Lauri Hornik have been the best of editors, always exacting, ever gracious, while Jasmin Rubero and Lily Malcom made sure no production question was left unanswered. Our agent Kathy Robbins and her team always know when to nudge and when to nurture. Appreciation to Ellen Goosenberg Kent, co-director of the HBO documentary *One Nation Under Dog*, for her counsel and friendship. We dedicated this book to our mothers, Lilly Salcman and Barbara Schwartz, with gratitude for everything they've taught us. But we also want to thank our husbands, Bill Abrams and Frank Weber, as well as our children, Roxie and Eli Salamon-Abrams and Remy Weber, who have given us gifts that can't be measured.

About the Author

JULIE SALAMON is the author of several bestselling and award-winning books for adults, including *Wendy and the Lost Boys*, *The Devil's Candy*, and *Facing the Wind*. She has written for *The Wall Street Journal*, *The New York Times*, *The New Yorker*, and more. She grew up on a farm in Ohio and now lives in New York City.

About the Illustrator

JILL WEBER has illustrated numerous books for children and adults, including *The Story of Hanukkah*, Sydney Taylor Book Award winner *The Story of Passover*, and *Cat in the City* and *The Christmas Tree*, both of which were written by Julie Salamon. Jill lives on a farm in New Hampshire.